nadiri, a novel

AMINA AL SHERIF

Black Rose Writing | Texas

ISBN: 978-1-68513-324-5
PUBLISHED BY BLACK ROSE WRITING
www.blackrosewriting.com

Printed in the United States of America
Suggested Retail Price (SRP) $19.95

Nadiri is printed in Book Antiqua

*As a planet-friendly publisher, Black Rose Writing does its best to eliminate unnecessary waste to reduce paper usage and energy costs, while never compromising the reading experience. As a result, the final word count vs. page count may not meet common expectations.

nadir — n

1. the point on the celestial sphere directly below an observer and diametrically opposite the zenith
2. the lowest or deepest point; depths: the nadir of despair

[C14: from Old French, from Arabic nazīr as-samt, literally: opposite the zenith]

possessive pronoun, Egyptian Arabic, meaning *my* ي- (-i)

Acknowledgments

Mom and dad- you have always worked your hardest to be the best parents you could be. I would not be who I am today without either of you. I love you with all of my heart- so much so; it makes it heavy.

To my childhood friends- Karim, Kylie- you have been some of the only constant aspects of my life. Our friendships mean more to me than you will ever know.

My beautiful daughter, Amal- someday, you will understand mommy's story. Be patient with me, and love me always.

Harrison and the crew at Writer's Ally- ten years is the longest relationship I have ever had with folks outside of those I just mentioned. You're why I'm here and why my story is being told.

Kirsten and Dr. John- thank you for your faith in me. Faith in my work. Your lovingness towards who I am as a person. I look forward to continuing our relationship.

Jenny, my creative godmother. I would be lost at sea without you in so many ways. You saved my life.

Last, thank you to Black Rose Writing for picking a Texan author with a diverse story to tell. Texas is better for it.

nadiri, a novel

PART I: SHAHADA

ولكاتبة هذه الرسالة أقول

لست اذكر من الذى قال صادقا

أن كل إنسان فى الوجود

مهما كان مستوى تعليمه

يستطيع أن يؤلف كتابا واحدا

على الأقل

إذا روى

بأمانة و صدق

قصة حياته

And to the writer of this message I say

I cannot truly recall who said

That every human being present

Whatever his education level may be

Can create one book

At the least

If they told

With honesty and truth

the story of their life

الكاتب عبد الوهاب مطلوع لأحدى قراءته ـالعصافير الخرصاء

The Mute Birds- Written by Abd El Wahab Matloua to one of his readers

The Interview
Cairo, Junior Year of High School

"Hagar Khalifa. Your name is clearly from somewhere else. What would you do if you were treated differently because of it?"

"With all due respect, sir, considering I am applying to West Point, I shouldn't think I would run into that issue."

There was a pause. The Skype bubble oscillated in and out.

Did they hang up?

The bubble continued pulsing- the call was still active.

Was that the wrong thing to say?...

Yes, Hagar. That was the wrong thing to say.

Oh, screw you.

The Senator's representative hummed on the line, breaking the awkward silence. "Well, of course," the West Point official on the line crooned.

A deep sigh hummed from her chest. Hagar looked up from her laptop, checking to see if anyone had heard her. The birds were chirping, the cream and pink flowers in the bushes next to her rustled their indifference. She had stepped out of class to take her first West Point interview. The heat of the Cairo afternoon beat down on the marble benches. Flies buzzed lazily around her head, and ears as sweat dripped from her forehead. She couldn't tell if the trickle of sweat was interview-induced or the pollution-laden heat.

Her attention wandered as the interview continued. All she knew about America was what she had read in books. Green everywhere- perfect grassy hills, mowed lawns, clean streets. No donkey carts or beggars, and no rubbish. No men in the street trying to cop a feel walking to school. Everyone was worldly and educated. America would have the fastest internet around with no state-imposed firewalls standing between her and watching the latest western movies and or listening to Western music... Cars that weren't held together with tape or rope. Nicely dressed people.

Best of all, it was miles away from Egypt and my miserable life.

Miserable, Hagar, only because you have made it so. Because you won't conform... Miserable because you will not bring your parents together- because you refuse to even pretend to be what they want you to be. If you were just less stubborn...

I'm the voice in Hagar's head. I negotiate with her every day, trying to pose logic against her emotional and often illogical thoughts.

After much discussion, she decided I should tell her story. She figured I would be the most impartial, the most objective and unbiased. Maybe having me tell her story instead of her would help clear the foggy memories laden with mood-driven emotional bursts and fight-fueled reactions. Maybe- just maybe, if she stepped aside and listened to someone else tell her story, the meaning behind the suffering would finally become clearer. Like early morning desert fog lifting on a winter day as the sun came out, the heat beating the life out of everything under it.

"Okay, Hayjar... or is it Hagar? I am sorry, I am horrible at pronouncing names... Thank you for interviewing with us today. We will let you know your submission status soon, and if we think you are a good fit for West Point..."

She smiled widely at the screen. Her heart sank a little.

You must be wondering- why is this high school girl in Cairo, Egypt interviewing for the premier military academy in the United States?

Maybe we should start at the beginning. Shall we?

Elementary school years

Every morning the students lined up on a field for morning assembly. They formed straight lines, each told to look at the back of the student's head in front of them, hands flat by their sides, palms against their thighs, squinting into the desert sun as it rose from the East. They wore uniforms, crisp from mothers cleaning and ironing them the night before.

Three whistles blew signaling the school principal. Hagar scrambled with the rest of the students to form straight lines, consecutive according to grade level. The students came to various phases of standing at attention, some still squirming with early morning energy. Teachers rushed down the lines for a last check before the morning's ceremonies began, pinching kids who continued squirming despite hushed commands to keep still and quiet.

Hagar looked back quickly in her line, stealing a glance at Hakim and Mercedes. Mercedes was right behind Hagar, with her hands softly placed on her shoulders. Hagar breathed in. Mercedes always smelled like flowers, even after long lunch breaks of running about the playground sandy and sweaty. Hagar smiled at Hakim a few places further back in the line. He gave her a crooked smile back. One of his two front teeth had fallen out. She giggled at his gap-toothed smile as he waved at her. Somehow a teacher pinched Hagar's shoulder and slapped

Hakim's hand down to his side at the same time scolding them gently to be quiet.

The Egyptian national anthem played from the loudspeakers. They all saluted, teachers whispering for the students to remember to bend their knees and breathe to avoid falling over or fainting. If anyone moved or talked, punishment would ensue during the first period, banished to a corner of the classroom facing the back wall.

A hum rose across the K-12 rows of students as they sang the country's anthem:

"بلادي بلادي بلااااااادي ... لكي حبي و فؤادي"

"Belady, belady, belaaaady... Lakki hoby wa fouaaaddyy"

When the anthem was over, Hagar glanced back at Hakim excitedly. They always read the fatha. Hagar knew the fatha as a series of memorized mumbles, sounds that skipped across rising vowels that would fall back to the grey corners of recollection.

بسم الله الرحمن الرحيم, الحمد لله رب العالمين. الرحمن الرحيم مالك يوم الدين, إياك أعبد وإياك نستعين..."

"B'esm ellah al rahman and rahim, alhamdullilah rab al aalamen, al rahman,al rahim... maalek youm el din, eeyyaak ya'bodu w eyyaak nesta'een..."

The school rested in the folds of the Wadi Degla valley, the lowest recorded point on the surface of the Earth. Most of the students were Muslim. But every morning, with the Egyptian sun rising behind them, every student, Muslim and Christian, stood quietly listening to the sounds of the nation rising and the Quranic verses of the *fatha* resonating between the wadi's walls. Hagar closed her eyes, pausing from stumbling through the last verse of the *fatha*. Then, her favorite part- a pause, a breath, a moment of reverence before they all closed the prayer:

"امييييييننن"

Aaaaaaaaaameeeeeeeeeeennnnn.

***

"I don't get it. Why did you have to do it? You just had to get punished during one more religion class?!" Bakry said. "Now I have to listen to the entire class talk about how MY older sister wants to be a Christian!"

"I just wanted to go with the Christian group because they have class outside and it was a nice day!" Hagar retorted.

They glared at one another in the back seat of the old family Jeep. They were driving home early after Hagar was called to the principal's office, which was becoming more commonplace. They called to have Hagar picked up early, andwhen this happened, Bakry and Hagar usually had to be picked up together. Hagar knew Bakry's mind was busy coming up with stories he would tell his friends the next day after they would make fun of him for leaving early with his disobedient sister again. Hagar's mind was also racing, wondering how she could show her face at school the next day after the embarrassing response the teacher said out loud to her seemingly innocent question.

Bakry, Hagar's younger brother, was born two years after Hagar. His frame grew to be small and delicate compared to others his age after he was born with mild Cerebral Palsy that caused his right arm to hang limp at his side and the fingers of his right hand to curl inwards as if cradling a stone across them. Despite his ailments, Hagar detested her brother most of the time- what he didn't have in physical prowess he made up for in manipulation and just...

Pure whining.

Yes.

Those looks mother and father would give one another when Bakry failed to hold a fork or spoon with his right hand and switched to his left... how he would come home from school and complain about how the other boys would make fun of his crippled arm as he tried to tag people while being IT…

Yes, and all the times they called YOU the hope of the family, excusing Bakry of any responsibility because he was sick…

I hated that.

Bakry looked exactly like his father. He had wide brown eyes and dark curly, coarse hair. The single inherited trait from the mother was his milky cream skin. This contrasted with Hagar. She took after her mother's steely gray gaze and dirty blonde hair. Hagar's complexion was dark, speckled with freckles echoing her father's Nubian heritage. A calm and non-confrontational child by nature, Bakry did what he was told. Hagar did not.

"People are saying you are actually Christian but will not be honest about it!"

"How could you say that?! You don't know. Nobody knows what anybody else truly believes! Besides, why shouldn't we be allowed to sit outside for Christian class, just to know what they talk about. It's almost the same as what we learn!" Hagar spat back defensively.

The Jeep slipped into a rut in the road, where a manhole cover used to be. The children cried out simultaneously as their curls smashed into the Jeep's soft top.

"MOM!"

"I'm sorry, I didn't see it!" the mother said, checking in on them in the rear-view mirror.

Hagar and Bakry looked at one another, rubbing their heads. Bakry grinned, his dark eyebrows leaping up on his forehead.

"Mom, do you remember when we got stuck in the mudhole on the way to school? By the bridge? And Hagar and I had to wait for the school bus?"

Bakry laughed.

The mother looked back at them in the rear-view mirror again, smiling.

"That was not a fun day. I had to wait until Dad came to pick you guys up, and you know how Dad moves. Slow as … mud!"

The children giggled.

Bakry's expression changed in the following silence. The temporary reprise from the current moment's conflict ended as he broke the silence.

"Mom, tell Hagar to listen better in Religion class. Dad will be so mad!" Bakry's eyes widened at the thought.

The mother's mouth transformed from the lingering laugh they shared a moment ago to a tight line as she shifted the Jeep into neutral, stopped in traffic. She turned around, looking at the children. A beam of sunlight streamed across her face, sand and dust swirling by her square jawline. Hagar noticed as the swirl of dust followed a piece of stray hair that had come loose around her mother's right ear. A blonde piece of hair.

One of dad's favorites, as he would say. Texas blonde.

"Listen to me. Dad will hear nothing," mother said.

"But mom, he has to! Hagar has to listen to the religion teacher or else she will keep getting punished and I will keep getting made fun of at school!"

"Oh, shut up. Mom, he is the kid here, why is he saying whether I should be punished? It was an innocent question, I didn't realize it would ruin our whole day!"

"Bakry, I will decide if Hagar gets more punishment than she already has. Do NOT say a word to your father, you hear me?" The mother's gaze shifted to Hagar; slumped in the back seat, pouting and looking straight ahead of her at the ground.

"Hagar, I don't expect you to tell him." The mother shifted the Jeep back into gear as they rolled forward.

Bakry slumped in his seat.

"You mean you won't tell Dad, just like you always do. You're always covering for Hagar!" he said.

"Shut up! Shut UP! I don't want to talk about it anymore." Hagar twirled a curl that had popped out of her bun around her right index finger. Turning her head, she stared at the donkey cart laden with fresh fruits trotting as fast as it could as the cart driver whacked its back with a stick. Hagar flinched with disgust, imagining herself leaping out of the Jeep and giving the driver a bloody nose for doing that to the donkey.

Deep down inside, she would have rather not been at any religion class, Christian or Muslim. But as early as nursery school, they separated children into different rooms for religion. That day, as they waited for instructors to switch from English to religion, she admired the beautiful day through the window by her seat.

"Christians, time to go outside," said the Christian religion instructor, who poked his head into the classroom as he walked past.

Hagar watched as a handful of the approximately sixty students stuffed in their classroom rose to walk outside. She turned to the window again; the sun beckoning her with its soft afternoon rays. She could see small afternoon shadows forming next to large pebbles in the sand. Then abruptly, she turned from her seat, stood, and approached the front of the classroom. Mr. Mohammad, the Muslim religion teacher, was rewriting:

"بسم الله الرحمن الرحيم"

"In the name of God, the holy and the merciful,"

At the top of the board. It aggravated Hagar that he needed to do this every time he walked into the classroom.

```
The last teacher still wrote clearly the
phrase in chalk, so why rewrite it? To admire
his beautiful penmanship?
```

She did not wait for him to finish writing the phrase.

"Mr. Mohammad."

He turned around, glanced at her, and continued to write on the board.

"Hagar sit down, class has not started yet."

"Mr. Mohammad, I want to go outside with the Christians."

He froze with his arm still in the air, stopping before completing the downward flourish of the letter *meem* at the end of his perfect line of calligraphy.

"What did you say, Hagar?" his eyes met hers in a stern gaze as he turned away from the chalkboard.

"I want to go outside," she mumbled, turning red. Her blood went cold in her arms. He misunderstood her, surely…

Well, or truly understood. She was so young, it's hard to tell.

"Fine, Hagar. Step outside," said Mr. Mohammad.

She waited in the hallway outside as he closed the door behind her. She knew he didn't mean to join the small group giggling and shuffling towards the door leading out to the play area. Peeping through the window into the classroom, she saw him pick up the grey phone on the instructor's desk and dial. The conversation was brief, and the next thing she knew one of the superintendent's secretaries was rounding the corner.

"Hagar," she said.

"Come with me."

Hagar walked slowly, keeping her head down as she shuffled to the superintendent's office. Her heart sank the closer they got to the top floor.

Hagar snapped back to attention as the traffic moved again. The man on the donkey cart cracked his whip, breaking Hagar from her reverie.

"The good news is," the mother sputtered and coughed as dust flew through the open window. "Hakim is coming over today, remember?"

All three sets of eyes met each other in a happy glance in the rear-view mirror.

"And your father will also be home after dinner to see us tonight."

Hagar looked back outside the window, her joy brief. Bakry's eyes twinkled with anticipation. "I can show baba the *hadith*[1] I memorized it today," he said.

Hagar rolled her eyes. Bakry was constantly showing off his *souras* and his *hadiths*. He was admittedly better at memorizing them than she was. Bakry loved Arabic and religion class and could memorize whole *souras* in just a few days. But the Arabic of the Quran did not feel natural to her. While she paid for her inability to memorize by standing in the corner in punishment for hours at a time, Bakry had his victory at the front of his classroom, reciting line after line to his awed classmates. She was not worried, though. She far surpassed him in math and English, which were considered the harder subjects at school by everybody anyway.

The mother pulled into their usual parking space across the street from their apartment building in front of the basket man's wagon. Hagar always admired the stationary wooden cart tumbling and overflowing with colorful wicker baskets. She always wanted to buy one so she could give a ten-pound note to the skinny man who sat hunched on a cement block who sold the baskets. It was curious; she thought- the basket man's concrete block seat was vacant, the man nowhere to be seen. Hagar wondered how his baskets were never stolen- it was as if the entire neighborhood had agreed to leave the old man's baskets alone, so he could sell them one at a time.

The mother looked at Hagar as the girl glanced at the basket cart. She could tell Hagar was clearly upset. The mother knew the look well. This wasn't the first time Hagar came home in low spirits.

"Bakry, go upstairs, take the keys," mother said. "I need to

---

[1] Prophet saying, or quote.

talk to Hagar for a second."

Bakry smirked at Hagar, taking the keys into his curled hands.

"Some-body's in trou-ble!" he said, scampering across the street and up the stairs.

Hagar and her mother watched as Bakry crossed the street haphazardly and scuttled up the stairs into their apartment building. Hagar began twirling her curls again, nervous. The mother turned to her, gesturing towards the concrete block by the basket cart. Hagar took a seat, and the mother sat next to her on an overturned basket.

"So, what happened today?" mother asked.

"Ma, I hate religion class. Mr. Mohammad gets mad at me all the time. And then I get in trouble. I'm just tired of feeling ashamed of everything I say," she said.

"Hagar, I know. You can't say things in class. It upsets many people, especially father."

"But why?" Hagar asked.

"Why would me wanting to be in the Christian class upset him? Can't I choose where I want to go? Or why couldn't I do both? And be half Muslim half Christian just like I am half Egyptian half American?"The mother paused. The corners of the mother's mouth turned up while searching for a response.

"Because, Hagar, you have to be one or the other."

The mother chose her words slowly.

"And right now, you cannot be Christian. At least not openly to your father. He would never accept it, and it would cause a lot of problems in the house."

"You mean, I can't be half-Muslim half-Christian? " Hagar asked quizzically.

The mother looked away, nodding with disappointment.

"No, *habibty*. You can't. It's not like being half American half Egyptian. You have to pick one."

"And I can't be Christian because Dad wouldn't like it?"

Hagar pushed further.

The mother shook her head, then placed it in her hands in a moment of frustrated thought.

"Hagar, your father doesn't believe religion is a choice," she said, trying another approach. "Since he is Muslim, you have to be Muslim, at least to him."

Hagar looked down. She knew the beliefs differed, but they felt the same. Both had Gods, even the same prophets. For Islam, Prophet Muhammad seemed to be the star of the show. For Christianity, Jesus was. But Jesus was a prophet in Islam, so why couldn't she be Christian? She knew her mother was Christian, and her father was Muslim, and that they did not always agree. But if they had the same prophets and both of them seemed to share the same God, why would it make her father mad?

And why don't I have a choice?

The mother shifted her weight forward on the basket and cupped Hagar's chin in both of her hands.

"Honey, one day you will understand. For now, you need to stay in religion class. Do your best, that will make us proud," the mother said, a forced smile on her face.

"Dad will never be proud of me," Hagar responded quickly. The mother stood up.

"Don't worry about your father. He will understand with time as well. Let's focus on having a good time with Hakim ok? He doesn't come over every day." The mother reached for Hagar's hand. After a pause, Hagar took it and lifted herself off the concrete block.

"Okay," said Hagar.

Hagar gave her mother a sideways glance. The family rarely had visitors at their house, because the mother had deemed the apartment not suitable for visitors. The father rarely liked boys visiting either, even if it was Hakim. Hagar and Hakim had been raised as brother and sister since birth, but Hagar's father had taken a firm stance against any boy coming into the house, even with the whole family present to supervise.

"Thanks ma," Hagar said.

But Hagar was having a hard time staying happy about Hakim's visit. It only filled her with dread on what would come tomorrow. They would all be waiting for her at school, making fun of her for getting sent to the principal's office yet again. As they crossed the street, Hagar forced herself to smile. If they weren't telling father about the incident, she'd better have a normal demeanor to avoid questioning.

The Family
Cairo, in the 1980s...

It might be appropriate to introduce the Khalifa family a bit more thoroughly…

Hagar's mother left America to fly from one hot dust bowl of Texas to another in Cairo, Egypt. She was all Stetson and Justins, her dark wavy sandy hair streaked with sandy blonde West Texas dirt. Her grey eyes held a steely gaze, strengthened by the courage from being thrown from the back of a bucking horse many times. The rodeo queen's memories of her younger years were filled with nights of driving down the drag on Main Street, making rounds for hours from the A&W on one end to the Dairy Queen on the other, and hanging off the sweaty back of some cowboy or another after a good barrel race.

The girl's father was born and raised in the heart of Cairo, on Al Manial, an island resting on the waves of the Nile River. His family origins stretched south and east- a mixture of Saudi Arabian Arab that flowed West during the Islamic conquest and the dark chocolate sweat of the Egyptian Nubian tribes, native to the continent. The father would tell her their family was of direct descent from Prophet Mohammed himself. The paternal grandfather radiated Nubian and African heritage in his portrait, the only likeness Hagar knew him growing up after he died years before she was born. Her father's mother was fair skinned, blue eyed Arab with dark red hair that reminded her of the deepest heat from embers of a low fire. Her father had climbed the societal ladder quickly, graduating from the prestigious *Kasr El Eini* Hospital's School of Medicine and became one of the most successful professors of Anatomy there. He would never tolerate ill speech about his country, his heart holding the deepest passion about his Egyptian heritage and roots. But the father cherished above all else the devotion of his heart and mind to Islam.

`Tell them why mom ended up in Egypt. People always ask me that.`

Ah, yes. Her mother married young, and subsequently traveled to Egypt with her husband as oil drilling expeditions in the Middle East prompted rotations there for most who worked in the oil industry. Hours that used to be spent massaging her horse with a round rubber brush, up and down and in circles, turned into the circular motions of scrubbing granite countertops, mopping marble floors, and occasionally entertaining guests in their large villa residence in Cairo.

Her mother would tell her stories of when she first stepped off the airplane onto the hot tarmac at the Cairo International Airport- how astonishing the desert was, how there had been no fences keeping the desert at bay, how small the airport had been. A hot gasp of wind swept the mother's perfectly coiffed bob. She would learn that wind was rare in the city, and would only blow strong during the dreaded spring months of the *khamasein,* the severe sandstorms that would drape the city in a red-yellow haze of heat and dust. This wind that tickled her jawbone and neck during her first moments standing on the airport tarmac was a gasp squeezed from the breast of the desert, struggling to welcoming Hagar's mother to a new chapter of her life with wheezing lungs.

`The mother would recall stepping onto a black-and-white striped curb to wait for the bus to take her and her husband to the terminal. The newness of the striped paint lining Cairo's sidewalk is an indicator of how recently someone` of importance had visited the area. Residents would know a dignitary was passing through when workers lined the streets in the never-ending heat painting the sidewalk checkered blocks of black and white. The bawaabs would sweep the streets clean and spray them down with water hoses. Growing up, I never understood why they watered down the streets. Being in the middle of the largest desert in the world this seemed ir-responsible and useless.

Remember, your mother explained that it was to keep the dust down in the streets.

Yeah, but then it would just turn into mud that would flick onto your clothes and stain them forever...

This curious habit would be one of the many nonsensical phenomena that would amuse the mother as she spent her first years in Cairo in a beautiful three story villa. Her first few years she was an oil wife. Her husband became consumed by work, gone for days at a time working at remote oil rig sites. In the long stretches of solitude and silence, without her horses to keep her grounded, the mother returned to school. Upon hearing about its prestigious status in the Middle East as one of the best schools for Medicine, the mother attended *Kasr El Eini* Teaching Hospi-tal. At this point she had spent a handful of years in Egypt, each day walking past the hospital's high concrete walls stained yel-low and its green iron gates peeling with paint. On a whim, she walked onto the campus one day and into the admissions office. Despite her inexperience in anything related to medicine, the college accepted her.

Probably because the man who received her ap-plication in the admission's office thought she was pretty, with her blonde hair and her blue eyes.

It was there she met Hagar's father.

At the time they met, Hagar's father had just completed a round in the intensive care unit as a plastic surgeon, reconstructing bodies after traumatic accidents like fires or car accidents. Hagar would later imagine her father transforming from Dr. Jekyll, a gentleman of science, grounded in logic- to Mr. Hyde, a man ranting of the apocalyptic times and rhetoric drawn from the Quran that seemed directly opposite to his profession. Growing up, Hagar was constantly questioning how the two sides of her father could co-exist in one man. In one moment he would rant and rave why she could not date boys, and the next explaining how without words the body communicated attraction through pheromones, drawing from everybody's need for the pleasure of sex. The mother recounted her father's doctorate research papers- marveling at how the father would weave snippets of the Quran and Prophet's *Hadith* as evidence of proof in his medical papers. In her father's lectures he would periodically inquire of his audience:

"Why do you think Allah made us this way?" or exclaim "Bless Allah, his creation and his majesty!" Often when a student asked a question he did not know the answer to, he would pause then proclaim, "Because Allah created it this way!" The mother would laugh at these responses. Somehow, Hagar's father wove the answer to that student's question in a later lecture. He was so good with his words, and would weave them so cleverly that the students would barely pick up on the fact that their professor had not answered the original question fully.

How could she not see it? The hints of disaster? The manipulation? The fascination with Quran ayyas as opposed to the truth?

The mother claims she fell in love with him the first time she heard him lecture. He claims he fell in love with her over fruit salad at a street cafe at *Khan El Khalili,* the sprawling marketplace where couples fell in love for centuries. Conceiving Hagar was an accident- while the mother's first husband wandered the

Western Desert searching for rich oil, her mind and body pulsed with fits of physical and emotional passion with the professor that filled the crevices of loneliness. Soon, the mother found herself wrapped so tightly in the professor's arms she could not let go.

And so, Hagar Khalifa was born.

Hakim Comes to Visit
Cairo

The girl and her mother scaled the stairs and stepped into the family apartment. Hagar felt a rush of relief as the door slammed shut- the familiar hollow but loud sound of coming home and the coolness of her bedroom waiting for her. She rushed to her bedroom before Bakry would dig at her more about the day's events, closing the door hastily. She walked to her window- it was her favorite part of her room. It was a large double-paned window that extended from the tip of her waist to a foot or two above her head. During the warm months she would open the curtains to watch families of birds nest on the outer windowsill, flitting amongst red blooms in the tree plants right next to their building. She spent many an afternoon gazing out of the window at the highway below.

Two highways crossed below her window, overlapping one another painting a gray "X" of asphalt that contrasted against the yellow of the surrounding sand. A tall brick wall lined an area to the left of the highway crossing spotted with watchtowers. That was Torah Farms. The locals called it *Mazare'a El Zeitoun* (The Olive Farms) because the prisoners bided their time in captivity farming the desert with rows of olive trees. From her window, Hagar could catch a small glimpse behind the walls, revealing sand lined with rows of struggling olive trees fighting the dry heat and pollution of the city. She had never glimpsed the prisoners there.

Hagar opened her door quietly and listened intently to see if her father had arrived yet. Silence greeted her, so she padded down the hallway to the kitchen to make herself a cup of tea. Since she could remember, she knew how to make a cup of *shayy belaban*[2] and a cup of Turkish coffee, *mazbut*[3].

Hagar walked back to her room balancing her cup of tea. She scoffed at a peculiar wilted plant that was growing from a hole in the ground by the front door. This family favorite detail of the house stemmed from Hagar's fathers' unhealthy habit of snacking on unripe green fuul beans. He would always with an air of pride, like he was trying to drown out the joke in his own righteousness.

Your mother would always joke that only an uneducated falah from Upper Egypt would eat raw fava beans from their own land that would then make them sick rather than nourish them!

One lucky *fuul* bean made it into the rather large crevice padded with dirt that lined the doorway leading into the living room. Eventually the bean sprouted a frail plant that grew to knee height, producing delicate wilted white and black flowers and more *fuul* beans!

Hagar closed the door behind her as she set her tea down by her bed. She immediately heard Bakry whining from the single bathroom the family shared, and she opened her bedroom door with a yank. Before she could reprimand him for being so loud he yelled,

"المیبة انقطع!"

---

[2] Tea with milk and sugar, a popular way to drink tea in Egypt.

[3] Translates to "just right," usually Turkish coffee prepared with one spoon of sugar as opposed to "zeyada" ("extra," or two or more spoons of sugar) and "sadah"-without sugar.

"Elmayya eta'ta'!"

Hagar rolled her eyes again. `Serves us right for com-`
`ing home early.` The family often forgot that the city would
frequently turn off the central water supply to certain neighbor-
hoods during the hottest hours of the day, when the family was
usually at school or work. This phenomenon seemed to happen
often at their house- more so than Hakim's.

"Use the bucket!"

"This is stupid! This only happened because we had to come
home early!" Bakry shouted back.

`Yep, there we go.`

When the water would return, they always had to run it for
a few minutes without using it, the sinks and shower spouting
brackish water speckled with black bits, coughing and spewing
as if ridding itself of a sickness. The toilet would flush only occasionally. Water was such a challenge in the house that the family arranged their schedules around its use. They could never
use the toilet when the washing machine was running. They also
couldn't shower when the washing machine was running, and
the sink would not produce water if turned on while either the
washing machine or the shower were being used. You get the
idea.

`Ironic considering the walls were full of mold`
`from leaky pipes. If only they could have routed`
`the leaks to our bathroom...`

Hagar could understand why the mother did not allow
friends to visit the family's apartment. She wondered why the
mother invited Hakim over this evening to play with the house
in such a perpetual state of disarray.

And speaking of which... Hagar jumped with excitement
when she heard a knock at the door.

`Hakim was here!`

Hagar followed Hakim down the apartment steps after dinner. They were going to go buy freshly squeezed fruit juice from

the shop downstairs. Hagar's mother had asked them to hurry back upstairs- her father would be home soon and would not approve of them being downstairs in the street alone together.

"A nice reward for leaving school early today," Hakim prodded, nudging Hagar with his elbow gently as they stood in line.

"Why do you do that? You know it makes your parents mad." Hagar looked at him sideways. He knew Hagar was stubborn and hard headed- but he always supported her. He was always on her side. Hagar looked at Hakim's face. He had deep brown eyes that reminded her of the caramel colored rocks she would hunt for at the family's farm in the desert. Compressed from years of heat, the rocks exuded a calm warmth with light, milky strands that would go around in concentric waves. His eyes did that too.

Hagar attended to the juice menu. Drink names were a mixture of bad English and the yearning for a life in a different place. "Magik" was a blend of citrus juices, and "California" was a blend of grape and peach juice. "New York" was a blend of deep purples from mulberry juice. Her gaze wandered around the store, examining the old tiling that lined the floors and walls. They were crumbling from age and probably hadn't been cleaned since the shop opened.

"You know why I do it," Hagar answered, breaking the silence.

"Hagar, push through it. We go to religion class because we have to. Nobody *loves* religion class anyway," Hakim responded.

"I'm sick of the school."

"Then ask your parents to transfer to the American school. You know mine would transfer me if you left. At least nobody would bother you and you could come home without getting in a fight for once. I would still be your friend."

"But I didn't get in a fight today," Hagar rebutted, crossing her arms as they approached the register.

"Yeah… you were lucky today. I wouldn't count on that tomorrow though."

Stop thinking about transferring schools. It will never happen.

Hagar sighed, her crossed arms sagging with discouragement.

"You know dad would never let me transfer schools though."

"Maybe he would."

It was finally their turn to order. Hagar ordered the New York City and Hakim ordered Magik. They received their drinks then walked outside the small shop to sit on the edge of the sidewalk.

"I am just dreading tomorrow. Going back to school. Hearing everyone make fun of me."

"They get to you. You can't let them do that."

"Hakim, I am tired. I am tired of the fighting. I just want everyone to leave me alone. My dad, people at school. Everyone."

"Not me, though!" Hakim grinned.

Hagar smiled in the middle of her sip of sweet juice when some stringy pulp spilled out the side of her mouth. Both giggled as Hagar wiped her face with a napkin.

"Yes, everyone can leave me alone, except for you," she said. "I *am* ashamed, though. There is always something each week. Some fight or something."

"Don't be ashamed, *ya* Hagar. It's just who you are."

Hagar looked at him, wondering if the statement was a good or bad thing.

The Pyramids
Giza

"Hagar, are you ready?"

Hagar could feel her heartbeat in her throat as she tried to swallow. Her inner legs tensed, her grip on the reins tightened. She weakly blurted out something between "yes" and "yeah", her gaze fixated on her mother's blonde wavy ponytail that danced in sync with the mare's thick, silver tail underneath her.

"Hold on," Hagar called out quickly in a shaky voice, pulling her light wash Levi's jeans up as she stood in her stirrups.

She knew they were near the Giza pyramids, but was not sure where. The desert always seemed vast until they rounded the next hill, the dunes curtains slowly pulling back to reveal the pyramids one block at a time. One would know where they were in the desert based on orientation to the pyramids and the direction of the sun. Smaller step pyramids were scattered all over the desert between Sakarra and the Giza pyramids, sometimes standing alone, sometimes in clusters. Some had revealed surfaces, perhaps brushed with the tools of human curiosity, and some were left for nature to continue stroking with winds filled with small, sharp grains of sand that would wear their steps away slowly over the years.

Hagar looked down after adjusting her jeans. She began calculating how hard the fall would be, if she were to fall. She concluded it would be a relatively rough fall because of the sprinkling of black pebbles that coated the ripples of sand, giving it a crust that would probably take off some skin. They weren't where the sand would cushion a fall.

"Hagar..?" she heard again.

"Yes, mom. Ready," she said shakily.

She watched ahead as her mother's horse trotted. Hagar's ride began trotting automatically, seeing its mate moving further away.

I hate this, she thought, immediately trying to hold the horse's back with the reins.

But it was too late. The horse had caught wind of the upcoming gallop and loped into a smooth canter. She raised up in the seat, taking a jockey's position higher on the horse's neck.

Then calm. Hagar relaxed as the horse transitioned into a gallop at full speed. The sand was soft and deep enough to act as natural brakes, and she could feel her ride's muscles beneath her pushing against the sand.

```
Then we would reach a moment of terminal ve-
locity- my body suspended high on the horse's
neck, the wind moving so fast by my face that
all fell silent around me. The horse's mane
would fly past me, the coarse hair dancing
alongside my own sandy curls.
```

They followed the crest of a hill. She glimpsed the top of a pyramid rise to her right as they turned. As the rest of the pyramids' geometry came into view, Hagar could almost count the large sandstone blocks. Then they rounded the crest of the hill to the top of it, and Hagar watched the early morning sun dance on the rough edges of the base of Mankawra, the pyramid closest to them. Contrary to many depictions of the pyramids, up close they were rows of large blocks, not smooth surfaces. The middle pyramid, Khofra, was also taller than the first in the pharaoh's attempt to dwarf his predecessor. The pair on horseback slowed, Hagar's gaze searched for the additional three pyramids at the foot of Mankawra- a little known cluster of tombs that brought the number of Giza pyramids to six rather than three.

I experienced this moment weekly but every time I saw the pyramids appear in front of me; the experience felt new all over again.

They slowed to a stop, the sound of the wind rushing back and bringing Hagar's attention to the surrounding desert. Hagar's mother turned around in her saddle gripping the back of the seat, smiling.

"How was it?"

Hagar smiled back. Her mother knew how nervous Hagar would become when they picked up speed during their rides. It was always rewarding for the mother to see her daughter's face, smiling after conquering a stretch of galloping at breakneck speed without toppling out of her saddle.

"Good," Hagar said as she tucked a couple of curls behind her ears. The desert always made her curls unruly. They stood straight out of her head as if charged with energy from the dry crisp air.

The mother and daughter concluded their ride at the stables sweating as the sun rose. After dismounting and handing the horses back to the stable hands, they piled in the Jeep and headed to breakfast. A small shop front with no seating and no name, the store had a deep frying pan by the doorway and a marble countertop with one man hastily preparing food. At ten o'clock in the morning, it crowded with local stable hands trying to buy a late breakfast after the first wave of tourists. Tourists didn't come here, hidden in the maze of sandy back alleys. Ignoring the men's stares, Hagar placed their order: four *fuul* sandwiches and two bottles of water. Men glared impatiently at the cook who was frantically preparing orders, wiping his hands on his soiled grey *galabiyya* in between sandwiches. Hagar loved the smell of the deep frying pan filled with a fresh load of grease. Recently picked vegetables arrived at the store at this time of the morning, all sitting on the countertop. Bright shades of oranges, green, reds and purples waited to be chopped by a boy about Hagar's age. After about fifteen minutes of cramped waiting in a sea of sweat, Hagar grabbed the sandwiches and headed back to the Jeep, crawling into the front passenger seat.

She wiped her forehead with her white t-shirt, turning her sleeve yellow, her sweat mixed with the fine desert sand. She ripped open a sandwich bag and ate the hot, steamy mush. The girl and the mother traded grins of happiness as the mother bit into her own sandwich, then rested the sandwich on the dashboard of the Jeep as she maneuvered the pyramid's traffic.

"Hagar, I have something to give you," the mother said with a mischievous glint in her eyes.

Hagar looked at her, pausing with a mouthful of beans. They giggled as the mother reached to the back of the Jeep, pulling a plastic bag forward.

Hagar took the plastic bag and looked inside. She smiled widely as she pulled out a notebook. It was a Moleskin- a kind of notebook Hagar had wanted for a long time. The mother must have had someone bring it back from the U.S.- Moleskins weren't sold in Egypt at the time.

"It's a diary. I know you love writing, and thought you would like to have one," the mother beamed.

Hagar smiled again.

"Ma, I love it," she said.

"Good, I'm glad," the mother said, satisfied.

The mother pushed the Jeep into first gear and drove home. Both were perfectly content riding in silence, basking in the early morning sun, each absorbed in their own thoughts as they made their way back across the Nile. Hagar closed her eyes and felt the gentle heat of the morning sun on her face as she fell asleep with her new diary in her lap.

Khawaga
Cairo

A powerful scent of Chanel n. 5 floated into the front of the classroom. A few minutes later, the superintendent strolled in with her assistant. Following behind them with a meek look on her face was Ms. Maha, the social studies teacher.

The three women stood in a single line at the front of the classroom with forty sets of eyes watching them intently.

"Kids," the superintendent said, her voice soft, high, and crisp. "I want to apologize for what Ms. Maha said about the Christians yesterday during your social studies class. She is here with me"- the superintendent paused, gesturing towards Ms. Maha, looking at the ground- " to apologize to all of you together. Talking about religions different from yours in this way is completely unacceptable, and we will not be tolerating it at this school."

The students' attention was laser focused on Ms. Maha, burning glares of accusation beamed her way. Ms. Maha was notorious for rapping kids' hands hard with her steel ruler, and she never held back any of her strength when this happened. Most hated her in the classroom. Hagar's eyes wandered to the handful of Christian students in the class, all clustered together at the front left-hand side of the classroom. They had their heads down staring at their desks, embarrassed.

The bell rang, indicating it was time for lunch. Hagar looked down at her uniform in dismay. The apartment had no running water for a few days now, and she was wearing the last of her clean school uniforms that she had. The uniform was too small and wrinkled. She was wearing a skort today- a choice that only the uncool girls in the class wore. Most of the girls wore skirts and somehow played in the playground with little fear of their underwear showing.

She left the classroom and walked down the round stairway to the assembly yard. There was a wooden verandah she preferred where she would write in her diary or read a good book. If she made it there early enough, they usually left alone unless the girl gang beat her to it. They would usually huddle there before a game of khalawis To her relief, the girls had already decided who was *it* and were making a break for it, laughing and giggling as she approached the verandah and they ran away. Hagar searched the group for Mercedes.

Mercedes had been keeping her distance from Hagar since the Christians incident. With each day that had passed since then, Hagar's heart grew heavier and heavier each time Mercedes ignored her. She never spoke a word to Hagar; but she could guess. Mercedes' parents were very religious- so to have Mercedes associated with an incident like that would be unheard of in their household.

Hagar watched the girls disperse for their game of tag wistfully, wishing she was with them. Hagar finally located Mercedes in the crowd of girls scattering away from the verandah. Mercedes was the furthest away heading to the corner of the elementary school building. She probably got a head start- she was almost never *it* first. Hagar stood under the verandah watching, imagining herself fleeing with them, likely paired up with Mercedes as they thought of the most clever hiding place they could find. Lost in thought, she almost fell over as the girl who was picked as it first darted under the verandah past her, having finished counting to ten on the backside of the wooden shelter.

"ايه يا خواجا"!

"Hey, *khawaga*[4]" the girl hissed as she brushed past Hagar, her frizzy curly brown hair brushing Hagar's cheek.

Hagar ignored her and sat down in the verandah. To fill her time. Sometimes she would write in her diary multiple times a day. Hagar fished around in her bookbag, looking for it and grabbing a new gel pen. After rummaging for a few minutes, a cold chill went down her back. Where was the damn diary?

Hagar shrugged and figured she had left the notebook back in the classroom on her desk. he hoped nobody would touch it, leaving it where it was. The teachers locked the classrooms during lunch, so Hagar instead opted to read *Mariel of Redwall,* a book her mother had checked out from the American school. She held the weight of the hefty 600 page novel in her hands, then cracked open the book and smelled its musty pages, closing her eyes in delight. She opened her eyes and scanned the playground and spotted Hakim on the slide with a few others in the class. He caught her gaze, waved, and smiled. She smiled and waved back. She suppressed a fit of giggling as she noticed one of their classmates sliding down the slide, hitting the notorious bump at the end, and falling into the sand face-first.

If there was one thing Egypt did well, it was playground sand. Raw and unfiltered, a child could get lost in finding interesting rocks and stones hidden in the yellow waves. I marveled at how none of us got sick after play sessions that involved the ingestion of handfuls of sand at a time.

Hagar heard laughing behind her. She turned around and saw the same group of girls who had scattered from the verandah earlier huddled nearby on the bleachers, their game of tag over. Mercedes was sitting in the middle of them with a

---

[4] Arabic for "foreigner", usually used in a derogatory way.

notebook in her hand- Hagar squinted, unsure why so many girls were so interested in a notebook. Then the hair stood up on the back of her neck as she heard Mercedes read aloud, - loud enough for Hagar and the rest of the little playground to hear...

"Dear diary... It makes me feel very lonely when Mercedes plays with the other girls at school and doesn't include me. They don't talk to me, but she does. Will I wake up one day and she isn't my friend anymore? How long will she be my friend...?"

Hagar blushed, turning hot. They had found her diary… She looked up and around to see Hakim's face as he froze on the playground. He caught her gaze and ran towards her. In a grip of anger, she rushed at Mercedes and the pack of girls, startling them. She hurtled up the first few benches of the bleachers, grabbing the diary from Mercedes' grip. Mercedes initially tried to hold on, ripping the first few pages out of the diary. The pack of girls scattered laughing with the pages fluttering behind them, the desert wind kicking up as if on cue, scattering pages away. There's no way in hell I'm getting all of those pages...

Ignoring Mercedes' cackling laugh, Hagar rushed towards the closest cluster of fluttering pages anyway, gathering them up as quickly as she could, fighting tears back. Out of the corner of her eye she saw Hakim gathering more pages that had fluttered away towards the spiral staircase. Hagar paused and stood up at one point, looking around to see if she had grabbed all the pages in the immediate area, wiping tears from her eyes to hide her crying.

Push it all down, push it all down…

She looked up towards the back of the building towards the section where the Middle School kids usually hung out. If it was possible, the shade of red on Hagar's face deepened even further to match her bright red pullover. There were a few of the Middle

School boys standing there, smoking cigarettes, laughing softly with a few pages of her diary clutched in her hands.

Don't go there…

Oh yes, I will, and I will tell them exactly what is on my mind!

Don't say a word…!

Hagar stomped over to the boys, grabbing the pages from their hands. With surprised looks on their faces, they burst out laughing upon realizing it was her diary that they had been reading from. Hagar turned to leave, hunting for pages. She paused, thinking of something clever to say…

But nothing came. Just a fresh burst of tears, and this time she was crying out loud, sobs and all. Wiping blonde curls from her wet, red face, Hagar turned and ran as quickly as she could back to the verandah.

Those kids were losers, hanging out behind the building in the alleyway. I knew what they did back there. When the playground monitors weren't looking, they would smoke cigarettes and throw the butts over the school wall into the desert. Losers. And a bunch of hypocrites too, how they would still smoke during the holy month of Ramadan behind the prayer tent when technically it was forbidden to smoke while fasting.

A colorful prayer tent would be erected during Ramadan in the same alleyway, used by all the same students to flaunt their piousness as they would break from class to perform all five prayers of the day. It was the unspoken rule that it was required for Middle and High schoolers to pray all five times. In elementary school, they were considered too young, still memorizing the required Quranic verses to get them through all the prostrations.

Hagar rummaged around in her backpack, stuffing the rest of her diary back into its pockets to protect it from the wind, looking to make sure all the rest of her belongings were still there. With tears still running down her face, she turned around and plopped on the verandah bench, her novel in her hands. She saw Hakim running towards her, with more pages in his hands. Her tearful gaze went past him to the rest of the playground, scanning to see where Mercedes and her pack of girls had run off to.

`How could she?`

Hagar jumped as the bell rang, simultaneous with Hakim's arrival with the additional diary pages. She shoved them into her backpack without a word, and looked down at her book, still closed and unread. She rose in dismay realizing she had not gotten to read a single word. .

All the schoolchildren crowded together as they made their way up the spiral staircase towards their classrooms. A voice whispered behind her left ear taunting her amidst the thumping of noisy footsteps scaling the stairway:

"Dear diary… today was miserable… nobody would talk to me!"

"Dear diary… I wish my hair was straight and dark instead of light so people would love me more!"

"Dear diary…"

She looked back. It was the same group of Middle School kids who were smoking in the back alleyway.

Hakim came running up behind her, slowing to her pace as she carefully made her way up the steps. He grabbed her novel from her hands, turning it over in his.

"What's going on? Is your book not good?" he asked, saying nothing of the diary incident. She didn't respond.

He whistled as he flipped the pages of the hefty novel.

"Hagar, how do you read these things? This is huge!" He glanced at her sideways as he handed the book back to her.

"You know, this really doesn't help you with the others… they think you are better than them, sitting on your verandah-throne with an English book this challenging!"

"Hagar, how do you read these things? This is huge!" He glanced at her sideways as he handed the book back to her. "You know, this really doesn't help you with the others… they think you are better than them, sitting on your verandah-throne with an English book this challenging!"

"I like the books," Hagar said. "And the Redwall series is an excellent series!" She sniffled, wiping her nose on her jumper sleeve.

Hakim punched her lightly on the top of her arm.

"Calm down silly! I'm not making fun of you! I know you are just a nerd at heart."

Hagar smiled as they walked down the hallway, waiting for the students ahead of them to file into the classroom.

"Well, today I am a nerd and more," she said. "An idiot nerd. Who keeps a diary that now everyone has read. Because I needed that after the incident a few weeks ago. I am a stupid, stupid nerd!"

Hakim looked at her, his eyes mixed with pity and doubt. He gave her a hug, right there in the middle of the doorway leading into their classroom so everyone could see. Good, kind Hakim was giving Hagar a hug. After hugging her he took her hand, and led her all the way back to her desk, his head held up in defiance. Hagar wished she could be as strong as him, but let her head hang in shame, tears still streaming down her face as the rows of students softly giggled as she passed by them.

The Farm
Giza Province

"Hagar," the mother said. "Wake up Bakry, it's time to go."

Hagar tried to shrug her mother's hand off of her shoulder.

"Moooommmmm, I'm too tired," she said, her voice muffled by the bedcovers pulled up by her nose. The mother scuffed the puff of Hagar's honey-gold curls.

"I know, Hagar, we do this every time. You can sleep in the car."

Minutes later after more whispers in an urging tone from her mother, Hagar slumped out of bed. After getting dressed, she went to Bakry's room to shake him awake. Unlike her, he was a morning person and woke easily with few complaints.

Fridays were farm days for the family. And this farm day was extra special: the family would receive its first Arabian horse. It started like every other farm day since Hagar could remember...

The family farm was acres of desert sand with signs of early desert farming- only a few acres planted at this point. She did not understand what enchanted her parents so much about the farm. About an hour and a half northwest from the Giza Pyramids, over 400 acres of pure desert belonged to the Khalifa family. Her mother told her it was her and her father's dream to have their own farm and live on it someday, and this was the beginning of their dreams. Hagar did not understand how this was her parents' goal. The farm was a dusty, hot experience that required waking up at five in the morning on the weekend.

Hagar would never admit how much she secretly enjoyed the car ride out to the property. The family sleepily bundled into the Jeep, the parents in the front and the children in the back, driving out of the city before the heat and traffic delayed them. The drive out of Cairo itself was uninteresting until the Ring Road. The road took them over the Corniche and the Nile, where Hagar would try to get a glimpse of the dark waters below.

She always marveled at how dark the waters of the Nile were just before dawn would break.It was the same Nile of the night, black waves reflecting the landscape's palette. A rainbow of lights from traffic on the Corniche, the twinkling lights of the small ferry boats and sailboats dotting the indiscriminate line that marked the water from the land. At the magical time of dawn,when the darkness broke, the Nile turned a lighter blueish black, as if its deepest secrets were rising to the surface, illustrating a soft story on the gentle waves to any onlookers awake to witness its narrative.

It was a stark contrast to the Corniche's daytime palette. The Nile would turn green as stagnant waters struggled to move against the pollution and heavy river traffic. It was swampy green, carrying in its folds the filth of the city. Water traffic caused some rippling waves; otherwise, the water remained stagnant and unmoving, as if heavy with the burden the city had given it to carry. People would park their cars on the sidewalks on cooler days and fish from the Ring road bridge. Street vendors in carts pulled by motorcycles or donkeys would plant themselves in the street next to the fishermen, selling smoked corn, roasted sweet potatoes and licorice drinks. Nestled in between those fishing would be young lovers attempting to hide from examining gazes, their fingers sneaking brushes past one another's hands as the only way for unwed couples to show affection.

When stuck in Nile traffic, these scenes appear beautiful,

paused in place. When traffic rolls out of gridlock, the frozen scenes merge into busy brushstrokes, as if Van Gogh had attempted to capture the movement of millions in the city streets at its busiest time.

Then the drive over the Nile would be over. Hagar would look over her shoulder, shifting in her seat, taking in the Nile's paintings for as long as she could before the next set of scenery. Lines of unfinished brick buildings that formed most housing in Cairo would then swallow the Nile from her vision transporting her to the Western banks of the Nile.

Bakry would sleep soundly next to her in the back seat. He would not wake until they arrived at the breakfast place. Hagar would catch glimpses of Bakry while he was sleeping, wondering how her brother was so different from who she was.

Her favorite part of the drive was next. For a moment, a clearing was large enough to see the pyramids of Giza, neatly aligned one behind the other. The sun rose from the East covering the land with a soft haze of pinks and light milky blues. She delighted in the pastel hues of the sky and her country's most prized heritage rising proud above the sand dunes, the sun's early light softly bouncing up the Pyramids's blocks as if steps, climbing higher and higher into the sky. For a moment, she was proud of her city and its heritage.

Then it would all disappear as the family took a right-hand exit off the Ring Road. Satisfied that she had stayed awake for her favorite part of the drive, Hagar would drift off to sleep. After a while, the Jeep would merge into the bustling traffic leading to Faisal Street. The mother gently reached back to see if Hagar awakened to her touch. It was almost breakfast time at their favorite place.

The Jeep came to a stop, and the father slipped out of the car to go order sandwiches. The same crowd of stable hands Hagar navigated after horseback rides with her mother were grabbing their breakfast at the same early hour. Locals would stare at the strange-looking family piled in the Jeep. The mother would look out onto the crowd with her ice grey eyes, not noticing any single glance begging to catch her attention. They would notice her fair skin, her hawkish nose, and her soft, wavy blonde mane. If they lingered longer, they would notice the girl in the back, with tightly wound blonde curls and dark skin. The girl's eyes were a deeper shade of grey; a cloudy day about to storm. And if the passers-by looked closely enough, they would then notice the young boy's head, with his brown curls that were slightly coarser than the girls'. If Bakry was awake this time, they would see a perfectly normal young Egyptian boy staring back at them, with chestnut brown eyes and milk-colored skin. As the father would return to the Jeep, arms full of sandwiches, the scene would come full circle, leaving many men wondering how this Egyptian man could find a wife so foreign and so fair.

Hagar and Bakry, both wearing soft sleepy expressions, would reach towards the bag as the father handed it back to them. Hagar pulled out two *fuul* sandwiches, craving the soft bean mash mixed with vegetables and spices. Bakry always chose *taameyya*, deep-fried vegetable patties with a layer of tzatziki sauce, shredded lettuce, and tomatoes in a pocket of thin, warm, soft bread. The children would mumble as they ate, a mixture of sleepy grogginess and blissful satisfaction.

By the time the Jeep had navigated the pyramids area and reached the Alexandria Desert Road highway, the mother would finally reach back to grab the parents' share of the sandwiches, smiling at the children who were fast asleep again.

***

They would jerk to attention at the farm's gate upon their arrival. Hagar and Bakry's heads popped up as the father honked the horn. A large metal pole that looked remarkably like a beam stolen from a construction site, propped on two cement blocks, comprised the gate that guarded the entrance to their land. The pole's lever and pulley system was a makeshift balance weight of more concrete held to the pole with a piece of old rope. This pulley system disappeared mysteriously into a small one room brick cellar. A piece of cloth hung from the top of the cellar's doorway providing the only protection between the inside of the cellar and the desert outside. Hagar wondered if the man lived at the gate all the time, or if he had family somewhere waiting for him in a proper home. Upon hearing the honking of the horn, the man would emerge from a small guard shack, smiling with his missing teeth, welcoming the family. He always wore bright galabeyyas. The father had built a small one-room cottage for the family to stay inside when they visited. The days were long and hot- the house had no electricity, and even less dependent running water than the family's city apartment. In the beginning, the family had no horses. But on this trip, they were receiving the first horse on the farm- a former racehorse the mother had rescued from their stable at the Pyramids. Hagar felt a mixture of excitement and apprehension. She knew the mother would want her to ride the horse as soon as it arrived.

"Bakry and Hagar, are you going to pray with me?" The father asked.

"Yes, baba, of course," Bakry said as he stretched, waiting for the mother to pull the front seat forward. Hagar rolled her eyes and said nothing.

`No, I don't want to.`

Shush! You might say it out loud one of these days!

The mother went into the house and began making tea as Bakry, Hagar, and their father crowded into the small bathroom to perform absolution before morning prayers. Hagar had always hated this ritual, mostly because she somehow always got her long-sleeved shirts wet from rinsing her arms to her elbows. After prayers, the family settled on the front porch to have their morning tea, accompanied by a pack of butter biscuits. Soon enough, an audible hum of a vehicle coming down the dirt road slowly buzzed to a crescendo in the family's peaceful silence. The mother looked over her shoulder down the road in excitement.

The father looked at Hagar, grinned and rolled his eyes.

"If we could crawl into your mother's mind at night, all we would see would be dreams of horses!" he said, his thick eyebrows high on his forehead. He threw his hands up then slapped his palms against one another, as if washing his hands of the issue.

Hagar and Bakry giggled. They loved it when their father would make fun of their mother, trying to get a reaction out of her. The mother wrinkled her nose, looking back at the father, slapping him playfully on the leg as she rose to get ready.

`I could almost imagine a time when they were truly in love.`

It felt like only moments later Hagar mounted the horse's back and was in the saddle, her mother looking up at her, beaming with happiness. The mother patted Hagar's leg reassuringly.

"Let's walk him about a bit to get him used to his surroundings, shall we?" the mother asked.

Hagar blinked, her body shivering with fear. She could feel the stallion pace energetically below her.

"Isn't this fun?" the mother asked enthusiastically as they walked around.

"Ma, why aren't you up here?" Hagar finally asked.

The mother looked up at her, a knowing glint in her eye.

"Because this is for you, Hagar. It is for you to enjoy!" she said. Then she pointed at Bakry and the father, both standing on the house's bare front porch with their arms crossed. "They will never understand," the mother said.

Hagar nodded quietly in return.

`I honestly don't get it either.`

"Be calm, and let him know who's boss," the mother said.

"Take him walking. Don't go too far out of sight. Just around the block, and you'll be okay!"

Hagar felt a flash of resentment, as her mother's cheerfulness seeped under her skin. She wondered if mother cared if she fell. She did not have long to think.

The stallion felt hot beneath her. It was as if his energy centered below her seat bones, radiating with impatience. She saw his curious and enthusiastic eyes on either side of his head as he twitched, reacting to every shadow cast across the sand. Hagar drew her reins in, threw a fake smile of courage towards her parents and Bakry, all standing on the front porch. She felt a flicker of triumph when she saw Bakry's gaze, filled with jealousy that Hagar was the center of attention. This fueled her shaky courage. She slowly directed the great stallion towards the only road on the farm, leading them away from the one-room cottage and towards the vineyards across the way.

For a few minutes, the girl and the horse appeared to talk to one another through small flickering movements, both equally full of trepidation as the other. Hagar's nervous energy led her to hover in her seat, mechanically stroking the stallion's neck. He arched his neck in appreciation. Hagar took his arched neck to mean one thing; that he was ready to run. Her nervousness rising, she drew in her reins. Before she knew it, they were trotting, ever so slowly at first…

He had a lovely, long stride trot. I could almost feel the joints of his legs popping as he extended them fully, eagerly stretching his body after a long ride in the truck that brought him out from the Pyramids. I rose and fell, posting with his gait, wondering if I had asked him for the trot. By the time I figured out I had definitely not asked for the change in gait, he had rolled into a canter. It was soft and loping, nothing to be afraid of. With each gait change, unbeknownst to me, I gave him more and more power. He was the one in control, and I was simply a helpless, nervous tick clinging to his back, yanking on his mouth as I drew in more reins to control him.

Maybe it was my relentless hold on the reins that irritated him, or that we had rounded another corner, headed back towards the house. A shifting dune in strong winds, energy flowed from his powerful hindquarters to his front legs. I finally recognized I was completely and utterly out of control at a full gallop towards the house.

The stallion didn't stop. He kept going, and a sick feeling settled abruptly in the pit of my stomach as the horse and I roared past my family, all watching in horror from the cottage porch. Out of the corner of my eye, I saw mother running after us. The last thing I remembered before the darkness was my mother's voice:

"HAGAR, HOLD ON!"

A New Well

The morning desert breeze was crisp. Hagar squinted as the sun rose. Soon, it would be hot as hell. But for now, the heat was tolerable.

Hagar turned her attention back to the house, lifting the bag of ice higher on her arm. She had fallen from the horse on her side with minor injury, despite falling at a rocky part of the road just past the cottage. The parents spent the rest of the morning examining Hagar for broken bones and bruises. She glared at Bakry as he prepared tea, throwing her a look of triumph whenever he passed her to serve the parents.

You failed!

After Friday prayers, at the hottest time of the day, the father asked Bakry if he wanted to go see the new well. Hagar wasn't sure what was more gratifying; the surprised-turned-proud expression on her father's face or Bakry glaring at her with anger.

"I do," I said.

"But baba, Hagar fell off the horse, she can't come with us!"

"Bakry, if Hagar wants to, she can come," the father said, ruffling Bakry's hair.

"She never comes on our walks!" Bakry complained still, pouting and stomping his foot, a tantrum slowly approaching.

"Bakry, straighten up!" the mother quipped, grabbing him by his upper arm and shaking him as she walked out of the cottage door onto the porch with a fresh bag of ice wrapped in a flimsy towel.

"Hagar is a big girl, if she feels good enough she can go!"

Hagar broke into a quiet grin, thinking of Bakry's face when the mother rebuked him. She waited for Bakry and the father to finish changing into their jeans and t-shirts after completing prayer in their white *galabeyya* they wore specifically for Friday prayers.

Bakry finally came outside and bounced towards the Jeep. Hagar watched him as he began climbing on the front of the Jeep, awkwardly reaching for the hooks on the hood with his limp right hand.

"I'm riding on top of the Jeep!"

"Only if Hagar rides on the front too," the father stated firmly. Both children noticed the father's face grimace slightly as he saw Bakry attempt to grip the front of the Jeep with his right hand's fingers, but could not grip the hooks.

"*No!*" Bakry whined, "Why do I have to do everything with Hagar! Baba I can hold on by myself!" he said as he showed his father the two fingers he had hooked onto the hood. His fingers limply threaded through the hook, unable to secure a grip.

Hagar watched as her brother turned to face the father, who was still grimacing at the young boy struggling. A pang of guilt and pity hung heavy on her chest as Bakry's expression changed when he saw the father's look of shame.

Dad was always good about showing when he felt ashamed of us. He couldn't help it.

Hagar began approaching the front of the Jeep before the mother stepped in.

"Bakry, it is because your sister is twelve and you are still ten. When you're twelve, you can ride on the front of the Jeep by yourself."

Bakry's face lightened up a little at that comment.

"Really? When I am twelve? You promise?"

"We will see," the father said gruffly as he glared at the mother.

Hagar hoisted herself on the hood of the Jeep and lowered herself down next to her brother. The Jeep let out a quick grunt as the hood dented in. Hagar and Bakry looked at one another, bursting into a fit of giggles.

"It was YOU this time, fatty!" Bakry squealed.

"Yeah, it's because I am bigger than you are- don't forget it!" Hagar said, grinning. For the moment, Bakry forgot about what the father said about his arm as he poked Hagar away from him, widening the dent on the hood of the Jeep.

The mother rolled down her window. "Hagar, please hold Bakry!"

Bakry rolled his eyes as Hagar inched closer to his left side. Hagar reached across him and gently undid his feeble grasp on the hood's hook. She grasped his small wrist and wrapped it around her waist. She could detect a pang of resentment and shame from Bakry, knowing it pained him that he needed help.

"Bakry, it's okay, let's have fun," Hagar urged, desperately trying to recover the moment despite her fall earlier in the morning and the dirty exchange of looks between them.

"It's stupid," he grumbled.

The father lurched forward as both children smiled, looking at each other excitedly.

"Hopefully it's a long ride!" Bakry said.

Hagar did not know where on their land the new well was being drilled on their land. That spring another chunk of acreage planted alongside the lonely block of vineyard right in front of the small one-room cottage. The father decided on mango trees. Farmers planted the trees straight from grafts, which were small and timid poking out of the sandy ground.

As they rolled onto the sandy gravel road and picked up speed, both children opened their mouths wide. Hagar looked back at her parents in the front. The mother leaned in towards the father deep in conversation as the father switched between pointing out of his window at the new crops and watching the road in between the children's silhouettes.

Another moment of love… Look, Hagar, they are not fighting.

Hagar turned around, taking in the desert ahead of her. The sand was vast, with speckles of tree lines here and there of faraway farms that lined their own land. Instead of walls, most of the farms planted tall desert pines and eucalyptus trees to delineate their property lines. The trees helped break the wind and slow the sand and dust on windy days. As they sped down the now sandy road, Hagar could hear the trees planted around their own vineyard swish in the wind as they drove past.

They finally arrived on the top of a hill. As the Jeep slowed to a stop, Hagar could see a small group of men, a white canvas tent, and what looked like a large tractor with a crane arm. She jumped down from the Jeep and started running towards the well.

"Hagar! Be careful, please! There is no fence, and the well is already deep!" The father yelled as he jumped out of the car quickly.

Hagar rushed over to the drill site and looked around her. The white tent was to her right. Large machinery huddled around a barely discernible hole in the ground. A handful of workers were between the tent and the machinery. A few of them lined up behind one another, all holding a large heavy white rope as if playing tug of war. They tied one end of the rope around a large pipe that pumped water out of the ground. The workers on the line had stopped what they were doing, looking at the curious little girl. Hagar's overalls seemed out of place amongst their light ragged clothing, her hair was tied back in a red bandanna with the blonde curls frizzy and wild from the Jeep ride spilling out. Her skin was dark, but not as dark as theirs. Her grey eyes exchanged curious glances with their brown ones.

Bakry and the rest of the family finally caught up to Hagar, Bakry running ahead of the family. Hagar turned back to see the pride in her mother and fathers' eyes as they gazed at their first deep water well. It would drill over 250 metres into the sand probing for underground water reserves that formed part of the Libyan watershed, the secret and necessity of desert farming in the Sahara.

"Is this one of the old drills?" the mother asked the father.

"Yes," the father said. "We didn't have enough to hire the new oil well drills. This machine will do- the crew here are very experienced. The men from the mosque recommended them." Hagar could feel her mother roll her eyes, letting out a frustrated sigh.

"Hopefully these men actually have farms of their own? You can't trust what everyone says at the mosque."

"Of course, what do you think I am, a simple *falah*[5]?" the father asked with a twinkle in his eye.

The children giggled as the mother threw her hands up in resignation.

He always evened the playing field with his self-deprecating jokes. Whenever mother tried to put a word in edge-wise, he would laugh her suggestion out of the way, joking about him being nothing but a humble falah. It was like...

Like he could use the term as an honorific instead of a diminutive. Like he was proud of his humble living (in reality he came from a well-respected class of doctors).

"Baba! Now you are a *falah* with his own well! Masha'allah!" It was Hagar's turn to roll her eyes, jabbing her elbow into Bakry.

"Suck up!"

Bakry poked Hagar back.

"What, Hagar? Do you even know what that means? Can you

---

[5] Arabic term for "farmer," oftentimes used with negative connotations indicating someone is not smart.

read what they wrote on the drill?" he asked in a mocking tone. He pointed to the well drill, its arm painted a worn yellow.

Hagar glanced up at the drill. It was awkwardly hand painted with flowers and Arabic script in the best penmanship. Almost better than what her penmanship teacher taught at school. The script slithered around the well drill in elegant script. Flower stems, leaves and buds outlined the words carefully:

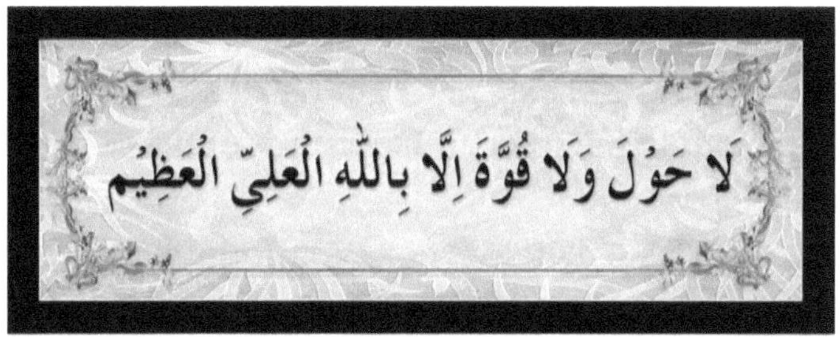

"*There is no power or strength except with God Almighty,*" Hagar said slowly, triumphantly looking back at Bakry's eyes then up to her father's.

The father's eyes lit up as he lifted his hands from Bakry's grasp to pat Hagar on the head.

"Look at you, my talented daughter. See mom? So we can't pull her from school," the father said in a pointed tone.

Why does he have to bring this up now?

"Dad, now is not the time to discuss these things in front of the children. I already told you she can continue her Arabic and religion classes as much as you want! Do we keep her at school at the expense of her happiness and health?" the mother said.

Bakry turned from the scene of the well being drilled and looked at his father, a worried look suddenly on his face.

"If Hagar moves, does that mean I have to move? Huh baba? I don't want to leave my friends!" Bakry whined.

"I hope not," Hagar grumbled under her breath.

"Hey!" Bakry punched her in the shoulder.

"Bakry, no, of course not. You can stay if you want to," mother said, patting Bakry on the shoulder.

"Why did you have to bring this up now? We were trying to have a nice day."

"Can we just not fight right now?" Hagar said in a loud whisper, throwing an accused look towards her parents. She had noticed the crew had stopped working again after hearing the family's exasperated tone and raised voices. She was sure it confused them enough seeing the family together for the first time. Inter-racial couples were not common this far out of the city. Seeing the mother was a shock, her light hair and eyes only seen in movies. The family having a fight in front of the crew would be even more embarrassing.

The family fell silent. It was not a comfortable silence, but one that held enough tension that the strong desert breeze could not dissipate. The subject of Hagar potentially moving to the American school had been a constant subject of fights and tension since the father came home for dinner the day Hagar was sent home early.

After the father walked over to greet the crew and exchange pleasantries, the family turned back to pile back into the car. The kids did not even bother asking the parents about riding on the Jeep. Judging from the look they gave each other, the answer was no.

Bakry and Hagar climbed into the back of the Jeep. Hagar glimpsed at her father's face, his jaw tight with tension.

"Why do you always have to ruin everything?" Bakry said as they rolled away from the well.

Hagar did not respond, watching the working men turn into black dots in the distance, lining the yellow sand.

Playing House
Cairo

Hagar stared at Mercedes as she stroked the small plastic brush through a doll's hair. The doll's hair resembled Mercedes' own hair- stick straight, silky smooth, with a slight wave at the ends. The doll's hair was bleach blonde, however, and Mercedes' hair was a pitch black.

The girls were on an uneasy playdate. The parents weren't aware that the girls had not spoken for weeks and had arranged for Hagar to spend a Saturday afternoon at Mercedes' house. As Mercedes continued to brush the doll's hair and the awkward silence hung between them, Hagar recounted the conversation she overheard between her parents the night they drove back from the farm the day she had fallen off of the new horse.

"Dad, Hagar is not doing well at school and we both know it. I mean, her grades are fine. But the girl won't make it if she keeps getting in fights with the kids every week."

She said nothing about getting sent home. Mom really can keep a secret.

"Mom- Hagar is there to do school, and focus on her studies. Her lowest marks are in her Arabic and Religion classes. She cannot move to the American school- she will lose *everything*. Everything that makes her Muslim, everything that makes her Egyptian."

"Dad, you know that won't happen. She will still continue

her Arabic and Religion lessons at home. She will still be able to study and continue Arabic at the American school. There is nothing to worry about!"

"*No no no no.* You know why Hagar cannot get along with children at school? It is because they all come from good religious homes raised with Arabic and their parents believe the *same* thing and they pray five times a day!"

"Oh dad, don't make this about me. You know that isn't the problem here- it's the fact that your daughter cannot come home from school without bruises from getting in fights and believing she has no friends at all!"

"You are her mother! You must raise her according to her culture- *this* culture, *my* culture! So she is having problems! She must stay in school, continue her studies, and improve the areas that are most important!"

Hagar was in the middle of recounting how her parents' angry whispers got louder and louder, more impatient when Mercedes finally broke the silence.

"Hagar, do you think you will marry someday?" Mercedes asked, looking up at Hagar's steel-grey eyes watching her.

"I mean, maybe," Hagar said, distracted by her thoughts still from recounting the night back from the farm. She paused.

Don't say it, Hagar, keep it to yourself...!

"You know, we don't have to get married." Hagar stammered as Mercedes reacted in surprise to her statement.

"Not all girls have to, you know. I mean..."

"That's not what my mother says," Mercedes cut in with her I-know-it-all tone. "Mother says someday I will grow up and have children just like her."

Mercedes' stroking of the doll became more tender, more sweet as her voice rang firm in its conviction.

"And you can't have children without getting married. It's literally impossible. Besides, wouldn't it be nice to have a nice house like this one and two little children of your own instead of playing with dolls your whole life?" Mercedes pointed at the Barbie doll castle she had towering next to her, placing the doll she had had in her hands on a lawn chair in the front.

Brought back to that moment of doubt, Hagar's thoughts were interrupted by Mercedes tugging at her curly hair with one hand. Hagar jumped slightly at the unexpected touch from Mercedes.

"What about Mustafa?"

Mercedes giggled. "He has curly hair like yours. You would have the most curly-haired babies!" she squealed.

Hagar shook her head.

"Mustafa is too religious for me…"

Hagar! Keep your mouth shut!

"Too religious?! Hagar, you can't say things like that! You know they are already saying things about you at school- how you aren't really a Muslim and that your mother is teaching you her ways as a Christian! If you had a crush on Moustafa and talked about it sometimes everyone would at least stop talking!"

"But what if I liked someone else?" Hagar asked with a tone of defensiveness.

Mercedes, about to retort a response defending Moustafa's religious piousness, paused suddenly. A twinkle crept into her eyes.

"Who do you like?" she asked.

"Hagar likes someone!"

"Who do you like?" she asked again, more demanding this time.

"Well…" Hagar stammered. "I like Karim. He seems like a really pleasant boy. He never gets put in the corner to be punished. Mustafa does it all the time!"

"Oh, Mustafa likes to joke! Besides, Karim is a Christian, Hagar. You cannot like him."

Mercedes picked up another Barbie doll, this one with curly, frizzy hair. She picked up a comb and started brushing the doll's dark, chocolate-y hair.

"But there are no Christian girls in our class. So who is he supposed to like?"

Mercedes was brushing the new doll's hair even more ruthlessly now, jerking out the tangles with all of her might. She glared at Hagar.

All of her little housewife dreams are just falling apart ...

"Your ideas are dumb," Mercedes spat. "I'm going to tell my mother. No wonder people make fun of you at school. You always say the wrong things!" Mercedes huffed out of the room.

Hagar stood up as Mercedes burst into her parent's bedroom. She saw the door to Mercedes's parents' bedroom open and close shut with a slam. Moments later she could hear Mercedes wailing and crying.

***

Hagar felt hot tears roll down her cheeks. She breathed in deeply, trying not to let out a sob until they were downstairs.

Her mother was angry. She could tell.

Hagar flushed hot thinking about what had happened. Mercedes' mother had rushed to call Hagar's mother, demanding Hagar leave immediately. Mercedes's father took Hagar by the forearm and sat her down on the sofa in the living room.

"You know, Hagar, these things you are saying are not correct," he said as he sat her down and walked back to the bedroom.

Mercedes's mother hung up the phone. Hagar had always noticed Mercedes's mother had an especially pale complexion, paler than most Egyptian women. Her cheeks were always rosy, her eyes always lined with the perfect mixture of black and light blue eyeliner. Her *hijab*[6] covers always perfectly matched with

---

[6] Hair cover, worn for religious reasons in Islam by women.

her *galabiyya* that she wore each day. Today, it was a black *galabiyya* with blue flowers. Each blue bud framed by two perfectly placed green leaves, picked from the most well-behaved plants.

Where are the stems?

Hagar, is that really something you need to be worried about right now?

Hagar waited in the living room on the perfect floral sofa chair waiting for her mother to come pick her up. Mercedes's father came out of the parents' bedroom without a word and began cleaning up the dolls and dollhouses. Hagar heard Mercedes' mother sternly reprimanding her.

"You are not to listen to anything she said, do you hear me? You are NOT to talk to her at school anymore!"

Hagar never heard Mercedes' response. Mercedes was still roaring. Hagar couldn't tell if it was from frustration, anger or sadness.

What was wrong with what I said?

Almost half an hour later, Hagar's mother arrived at the door, greeted by Mercedes's father's stern and upset hushed words. The mother brushed past him and quickly grabbed Hagar by the arm. The girl rushed to her mother when she saw her, as if she had been sitting alone on the floral couch for hours. Mercedes' father escorted both of them to the stairwell.

"I am so sorry, this is a massive misunderstanding," he apologized to Hagar's mother as he ushered them out the door.

"The girl is young, I am sure she did not mean what she said."

"I will figure out exactly what they said when I speak with her," Hagar's mother responded sternly. And that was that.

Mercedes's father squirmed uncomfortably, glancing back at Mercedes's wailing still ongoing.

"I think we need a break for a while."

"A break? The girls are best friends. What do you mean a break?"

His caramel colored eyes darted from side to side.

"I don't think the girls agree on how the world works."

He paused.

"How our world works. It's better for Mercedes to spend time with girls aligned with our family's beliefs. Hagar is a good girl, just not for our daughter," he concluded hastily.

He looked at Hagar as if he knew the girl should not be within earshot for the rest of the conversation.

He paused.

Hagar stared through him, her grey steel eyes filled with tears.

`More aligned?`

`A break?`

`But she is my friend.`

"Don't worry, I will take care of this," Hagar's mother continued. "Just please, leave my husband out of this. He has enough going on at the hospital and really does not need to be worried by this."

Mercedes's father nodded quickly, beginning to retreat into the house. "Of course, of course, we do not want any trouble."

Hagar's mother yanked the girl away from the front door, her grip on Hagar's arm still firm. The two piled into the white Jeep, and were silent all the way home.

***

The pair arrived home with a sigh of relief seeing that nobody else was in the house. Bakry played tennis with Mercedes' younger brother Omar on Saturday afternoons and was still at the sporting club. Hagar rushed in the front door and headed straight for her room. She sat on the bed, her eyes red from crying silently all the way home.

The mother opened the door. Her anger and frustration aside, she scooted onto the bed to sit next to Hagar.

"How are you feeling?" the mother asked.

"I don't know," she shrugged.

The mother sighed and put her arm around Hagar, pulling her in close. "Honey, you will sometimes lose friends. That's part of life."

"But I still don't understand what made Mercedes so upset."

"Honey, we have been over this already. Some people cannot look at things differently like you can. And she doesn't understand religion in the way you do. She is like Dad and Bakry. You cannot reason with that, you just have to accept it."

"That's fine, but why can't they just accept me, then?" Hagar demanded defiantly.

"Because, honey. Your opinions are hard to hear for them. They are hard to understand. You are questioning everything. And asking questions about things that people believe so strongly is hard for them to hear without anger. "

"I still don't get it. School tomorrow is going to suck."

The mother sighed. "Hagar, you will be fine. Get through this. Get through this."

"Mom, what about next year? Can I move schools? Can I go anywhere else?" Hagar asked, her voice pressing and desperate.

"Let's take on next year when it comes."

She twisted to open the top drawer of Hagar's nightstand. The mother pulled out a blue Bible. Hagar stared at her mother as she read by the lamplight silently.

"Ma," Hagar said softly. "Can you read to me?"

Her mother looked over to her and smiled. "Of course, honey."

And she read.

That's It
Cairo

Hagar hit the ground on her knee, hard.

Why did they choose the one concrete spot? They could have at least picked the fight on the grass. Or in the sand.

"Who is going to pick you up *now*, Hagar?"

"Where's your mommy? Is she going to come to pick you up from school early again?" another voice rang out in singsong.

Hagar stood up slowly and spat on the ground. Blood.

"*Fuck you,*" she said in English. Mercedes stood, her arms crossed, a smirk smattered across the soft skin of her face. "Or do you idiots even know what that means?"

"We understand your stupid English," one said pointedly. "Go somewhere else and use it, *khawaga!*"

"I am not a *khawaga!* My father is an Egyptian *falah,* more Egyptian than any of you!"

Snickers.

"Is that where you get your blue eyes and light hair?"

"Do you tell your daddy that you want to hang out with the Christians?"

Students started standing around the location of the brawl. Hagar knew it would only be a matter of time before a playground monitor would come running around, blowing her whistle.

"Hagar, you *are* a khawaga. Even the Christians won't talk to you," Mercedes spat. "Even Yung, and he is from Vietnam! He is more like us than you are!"

"Why? Because he can barely speak English?" Hagar retorted. A few students shook their heads in disapproval, whispering to one another.

Two whistles blew, sharp and short.

"خلاص! اه ده! بطلوا يا جماعة!"

"Enough! Stop it you guys!"

A playground monitor came rushing towards the crowds. Hagar looked behind the monitor to see Hakim, standing with his hands covering his mouth. Mercedes and her crew along with the bystanders dissipated.

"Hagar, look at you! What have you done to yourself?"

The playground monitor brushed dust from Hagar's skirt.

The playground monitor screeched, brushing dust from Hagar's skirt.

"It wasn't me!" said Hagar, wincing as the playground monitor grabbed her arm to pull her up off of the ground. "It was *them!*" She pointed at Mercedes and the girls as they ran up the spiral staircase towards the classroom.

"They did this to me!"

" Oh, surely," the playground monitor murmured, still holding onto Hagar's arm. "It's always them. Come on, principal's office!"

***

"Oh jeez, Hagar," the mother said as she rushed into the principal's office. She kneeled next to Hagar's chair, examining the girl's nose and face. She took Hagar's hands, opened them sideways to see the girl's knees, which were skinned badly.

Ms. Aisha stood up behind her desk. She had been patiently waiting for Hagar's mother to arrive. Hagar had watched the principal as she elegantly clicked about the computer desktop that sat on a reddish-brown heavy looking desk. Two large plants framed the principal on either side of the desk towering behind her, picture frame-like. The school nurse, who had been called to help clean Hagar's cuts, had sat Hagar down in one of the two stiff chairs facing one another in front of the principal's desk. Hagar was staring at the empty chair in front of her when her mother had rushed in.

"I gave her a juice, I hope you don't mind," the principal said softly, gesturing for the mother to sit down in the chair opposed to Hagar's.

The mother sat at the edge of the seat, her eyes scanning her daughter from head to toe. *Yep- one eye would definitely turn into a black eye,* now just swollen shut and glinting red. Both of Hagar's cheeks flushed red- the right side of her face bright with blood from where she must have scraped the concrete face down. Judging from the amount of bandages she assumed the knee injury wasn't a minor wound.

"Ma'am, I am so sorry this keeps happening. I don't know what to say." The principal's voice was soft with an edge of anxiety. "And you know how it is at this age- it's so hard to figure out who started it. I am sure Hagar was just voicing her opinion like she usually does."

The principal paused, then turned to the mother. "I thought Mercedes and Hagar were best friends. What happened?"

The mother shook her head.

"Maybe children have a hard time resolving differing opinions just as adults do."

The mother stood up, motioning for Hagar to do the same.

"I think it is time to take her home," the mother said. Hagar eagerly stood and took her mother's hand in her own.

Ms. Aisha stood as well. "Of course," she said. Both of her soft white hands were wringing one another in nervous tension.

"Ma'am... may I advise you to consider... Maybe Hagar

needs to move to a different school. Maybe even just for a while until these… thoughts in her head are sorted out with… the family, you know?"

"I will discuss with my husband," mother said.

Ms. Aisha nodded in agreement. "It is for the best," she said.

Hagar looked up at her mother hopefully. Is she really going to get me out of here?

Yes, but it will not get any easier, sweetheart.

They both walked out. The courtyard was quiet with everyone back in class. Hagar still looked left and right, looking for any sign of people from her class who might spot her leaving early yet again, this time bandaged up in defeat. The girl and the mother walked to the whitewashed front gate and out onto the street. Hagar felt a wave of relief as they approached the white Jeep.

It was supposed to end there.

***

I went back to school. For a few weeks. It was as if they ordered everyone there not to talk to me. Things were peaceful, at least for a while. At home, they were not.

I was riding in the Jeep. Father was taking me to school. There was a clear silent tension as we listened to the Quran on the local radio.

Mercedes never came back to school after the fight. Apparently, her parents had pulled her out of school that day. They figured she would do better at a more religious school, one that would instill their ideals of a good Muslim girl rather than the raucous consequences of a too-diverse student population. I overheard father talking about Mercedes' transfer. He insisted I go to a similar school- a madrassa- to learn the words of God. Maybe that would make me get along with my peers better. Maybe I would actually have friends, he added insistently. But it would make me into the proper, obedient Muslim daughter that I was, not the ornery disobedient heathen that I was becoming.

Mercedes' family car was one I couldn't forget. A maroon Volkswagen Polo. One day on the drive to school I spotted a car that looked familiar, driving ahead of us on the dusty gravel road. I sat up, and squinted to look into the car. It had to be hers.

As traffic lurched to a congested stop, I peered at the car. A woman wearing a hijab was sitting in the front passenger seat- she looked just like Mercedes' mother. A man was sitting in the driver's seat. But it looked like a small head covered in hijab was sitting in the back seat, rather than the expected soft silky black hair.

Maybe I was wrong, maybe it wasn't her. Mercedes didn't wear hijab.

As traffic moved, I slumped back. I kept an eye on the car ahead of us, still hopeful. Maybe it was Mercedes; she was finally coming back to school. I saw the woman in the front seat gesturing aggressively, then turned around, reaching for the back seat. I could not see her face, but she appeared to be adjusting a black hijab wrapped around a small head in the back seat. I peered even closer, secretly urging my father to drive faster so we could get a better look. Was it her?

But it was too late. The maroon car peeled to the right. My father noticed in the rear-view mirror.

"You know ya Hagar, there is a really nice all girls madrasa down the road. Maybe we should look at that for you rather than the American school. Huh?"

I never responded. I was still following the maroon car until it disappeared beyond the yellow, gravelly road.

Part II: Salat (Prayer)

One night I dreamed I was locked in my father's watch
With Ptolemy and twenty-one ruby stars
Mounted on spheres and the Primum Mobile
Coiled and gleaming to the end of space
And the notched spheres
Eating each other's rinds
To the last tooth of time,
And the case closed.

— John Ciardi, The Collected Poems

New Beginnings
Cairo
Middle School Years

Hagar looked down at the selection of clothes spread out on her bed.

What to wear? That was the most important question of my Middle School years.

It had been two years since she had transferred to the American school. There, they had no uniform- only a dress code. Kids wore whatever they wanted to school! It was a cause for joy initially... until Hagar realized how scant her wardrobe really was.

She had to hurry- she had to get to youth group. A small group of friends she had made at school had invited her to a church's youth group. Most of the kids who attended went to the American school. Mostly expats, there were a handful of locals who attended too.

It amazed me how long it took to choose your outfits... it still took you at least twenty minutes to try clothes on and decide!

Well, I had to look my best for the occasion. But not look like I was trying too hard. It was a tough balance to manage.

Two outfits laid in front of her. One was a 3/4 length grey henley shirt coupled with a pair of shorts, both hand-me-downs from Grace. Her friendship with Grace grew from an old family relationship. Grace's mother and Hagar's mother had grown to be friends long before the girls were born. Hagar vaguely re-called a few playdates with Grace when they were much younger, but the friendship drew to a pause once Hagar began at the local school. Once transferred to the American school, it was a natural fit for her and Grace's lives to converge.

Hagar stared at the two outfits she picked out for the evening, undecided. Grace's mother sent Grace's old clothes to bolster Hagar's wardrobe. The shorts were short for Hagar. She had never worn them outside of the house. She felt daring tonight, so she decided on that outfit before looking at the other one more time.

The other was a pair of Levi's jeans with a black t-shirt. Hagar balked at the idea of wearing jeans in this heat. Heat or no heat, Hagar's mother wore jeans every day. Hagar wondered why her mother never wore shorts, ever, but decided against asking. She felt a rush of nervous happiness as she slid the shorts on, her legs bare beneath her.

She peeked around the corner past the door. Seeing no one in the hallway, she grabbed her bag from next to her nightstand and walked out confidently.

"Hagar, what are you doing? Where are you going?"

She froze as she turned to see her father standing in the hallway behind her. She didn't know he was home. Dropping her bag, she braced herself for what was coming.

"Dad, she's going to Grace's house to study," the mother said from the kitchen, poking her head out of the doorway so her voice could reach the father at the end of the hall. The mother's gaze shifted to Hagar's legs. She shook her head when she saw Hagar's outfit.

"You're going to walk in the street like THIS?"

I hated it when my father did this to me. All the other girls at my school would wear shorts even shorter to school and walked in the street. Part of me thought that if he just left it alone, and didn't make such a big deal out of my legs, then maybe the significance of their bareness would disappear entirely.

"Hagar, answer me!"

The father's voice escalated, demanding the girl's attention.

"You think you are going to bare your legs like a prostitute in the street?!"

The mother's eyes widened. "Now, that's enough! It's just a pair of shorts!"

Hagar looked down at her legs.

Are my legs ugly? Is that why dad was trying to cover them up? Was he ashamed of them? Should I be ashamed of them?

Why wasn't anyone allowed to see my legs?

"Dad, if anyone is looking at my legs like that, they should go to hell for having those thoughts in the first place!" Hagar retorted. "Besides, they pass school dress code and all the girls wear shorts!"

Her father's eyebrows shot up."You bring shame to this family!"

"And you would cause men to think sinful thoughts? Hagar to put yourself outside like that, a temptation to good men, is haram!" "Ever since she moved to this American school, she does not listen! At least there she was doing good by her heritage and by Islam attending religion class every day, and wearing a uniform instead of- dumb things!" The father sputtered.

"Change your clothes now! And give me those shorts when you are done!" He said, motioning her back to her room. "You should not be allowed to go to Grace's house at all!" [7]

"They have to do a project together. Hagar has to go," the mother insisted.

The father glowered. "Hagar, give me those shorts when you

---

[7] Quranic verses.

change into something more respectable," he repeated.

Hagar slammed the door shut. She could feel tears coming to her eyes, but she pushed them back. Why couldn't she wear what she felt like wearing? And why was everything she did wrong in his eyes? Why did her father hate everything she did?

She skulked to her closet. `I need approval from no one. Someday, I'll go to America. There, nobody will judge me for wearing shorts.` She pulled out her previous outfit- her pair of Levis and her black shirt- and pulled them on; the shorts dropping to the ground. They slumped by her ankles, lifeless on the floor. She laid the shorts on her bed, looking at them forlornly. Her father would probably throw them in the trash.

She opened the door and could hear the shouting in the parent's bedroom. `Father picked a fight. What a surprise.` For a moment she paused, worried about her mother.

She had to make sure her mother was okay.

She grabbed her shorts and headed towards the parent's bedroom door.

"Ever since she moved schools… why? She is our daughter, the same daughter as she was at the old school!" Her mother pleaded.

"Yes, that is exactly the problem!" Her father's voice resonated with anger.

"She is the same, and now worse! She acts like them, thinks like them and now dresses like them? I will go to hell for her acting like this! God will punish me for her actions"

"Get out!" Her mother said.

"I want no more of this. We can never have peace when you come home. I am tired, she is tired, leave us alone!"

Hagar backed away from the door slowly.

`The fights had gotten so much worse since I had moved schools. Mother did everything she could to hide it from us… But father had no` qualms with showing his anger at the decision.

"You don't need me? Huh? *You don't need me!*" The father yelled back. "Fine, I will leave you both! You can do this on your own without me!" Hagar heard the shatter of glass, and without hesitation opened the door and rushed into the bedroom. He had slammed his fist into the mother's closet. A mirror lined each of the closet doors, tall and long. Hagar and her mother would pass long, scorching afternoons making funny faces giggling at the mirror. His fist landed in the middle of one of them, cracking it to crumbling pieces.

Without looking at his hand, which was now dripping with blood, the father turned to storm out of the bedroom. Seeing Hagar, he reached out for the shorts, snatching them from her hands and almost knocking her to the floor. The mother rushed to grasp Hagarin her arms. The father stomped down the hallway. Hagar watched as his silhouette turned into the kitchen.

"These shorts! All things haram! They will not be in this house!" the father said. Hagar and her mother heard the gas stove turning on. What was he doing? Hagar's mother let go of the girl and rushed to the kitchen door. Was he burning down the house?

Hagar scrambled behind her mother, not wanting to be left alone. Both of them peered into the kitchen just in time to see the father light the shorts on fire. He dropped the shorts on the stovetop flame as it soared up close to his fingers. He watched with satisfaction as the shorts burned.

"Dad, *what are you doing?*" the mother said as she rushed into the kitchen, turning the sink on to fill a bowl with water. "You will burn the house down!"

"If the house burns then rightfully so- the flames of hell will burn this family down as we deserve!"

Despite his forceful anger, he stepped aside to allow the mother to turn off the burner and douse the shorts with water.

"Hagar, just *go!*" The mother said. "Your father and I will handle this. Do *not* be late!"

Hagar felt burning guilt. She knew all of this was because of her- because she had worn the damn shorts. If she had just pushed them aside, pushed that *stupid, awful* urge to wear those shorts aside, none of this would have happened.

She rushed to her room, grabbed her bag, and slammed the front door.

Walking in the Streets

Cairo, Egypt

Her mind would churn with anxious thoughts, and nervousness as she walked to youth group.

This was not the first time she had been to youth group, but she couldn't recognize everyone there. She visualized the expression she would wear in her mind as she moved through the throng of Middle and High Schoolers. She didn't want to show how lost she felt looking for Grace, the only face she knew amongst the crowd. Her biggest worry was being left awkwardly standing around by herself until someone took pity and talked to her.

As she walked, she mentally prepared herself to greet people there, pretending to be happy, and trying to forget what had just happened at home. She could feel herself sweat from the early evening heat, droplets rolling down the insides of her legs. So I wanted to wear the fucking shorts. So I wouldn't show up swimming in my sweat. She marveled at how a country like Egypt could stifle its own people by making them cover every single part of their body. Maybe that is why dad is cranky all the time- because he is too hot. She scoffed at the thought. She knew that by the time she arrived at the youth group event, she would probably soak wet with sweat.

She kept her head down when she walked in the streets. She

knew what would start the moment she left her apartment building- that feeling of being watched. Every set of eyes would turn to her on the street. Everything about her appearance and demeanor screamed "I'm not from here!" She remembered venting to Hakim once, asking him what about her looked foreign. "It's… the way you carry yourself," he had responded. "No Egyptian woman walks around like you do. I don't know. You don't walk like an Egyptian woman!"

Hagar marveled at this thought, still trying to figure out what "walking like an Egyptian woman" looked like, when she started hearing the voices.

"اه ياقمر تعالي اقعدي معي شويه!"

"Hey pretty lady. Come sit with me for a bit,"

"شعرك جميل, واووو!"

"Your hair is beautiful, WOW!"

"إديني عينك ياعسل"

"Give me your eyes, honey"

"بس هي بتمشي ازاي بتحرك طيزها كده المفروض البت دي تفضل محبوسة في البيت!"

"Look at how she is walking, shaking her ass like that. She shouldn't be allowed out of the house."

With each cat call, her burning rage would mount. Sometimes she could ignore them. But tonight, she couldn't shrug them off. In the shadows of the late evening, she tried to face the voices- identify them, make eye contact with them. But when it was even slightly dark outside, it was hard to identify the men who owned the voices- they all seemed to hide in the shadows, the glow of their cigarette butts like fireflies in the dark. Not like the sharp yellow daylight mattered when she walked during the day- they still catcalled her. But during the daytime it was easier to ignore them in the bustle of traffic. At night, there was something about the totality of the desert darkness that made things slow down into an electric hum waiting for something to pop a spark.

"بس الرجلين دول"

"Look at those legs…"

Like rabid dogs, those motherfuckers. I hated them so much. And every day I would have to endure them, every corner I turned, every place I tried to go. Old and young, they would taunt me.

Policemen were the worst. President Hosni Mubarak enacted emergency law when he took power of Egypt, and this law required stationing policemen every 100 meters in populated areas to "enforce the law". They never actually did that.

The policemen didn't stop others from following Hagar. Men gathered at the bodega by her house smoking and dealing drugs- it was a well-known spot. The police were involved too- the throngs of young men never went away. The police stand at the bodega was almost always empty. If a policeman was there at night when the crowds would show up, they would simply sit and smoke cigarettes, having a casual conversation with the surrounding men in various states of high.

I would dream of hurting them. Punching one of them in the face, or maybe kicking them in between their legs. Making them scream. Scratching their faces until they bled, and her nails were full of their dirty looking skin.

Sometimes she would flip them the middle finger and they would laugh. She would yell Arabic curse words back at them. Sometimes this would silence them. She could almost feel their questioning: *How does this foreigner know Arabic?* Sometimes, it would egg them on.

She rounded the corner, almost at the building where youth group was being held. She was far away from home now. The evening had turned into night and the dark corners took over the sidewalks with shadows.

Then, she heard her favorite one:

"خواجة يا جميلة يا خواجة"

"Khawaja, pretty khawaja"

But this was closer than she expected, the breath from the

voice brushing against her ear.

She turned to face the shadows. She saw the outline of the police stand first- an iron chair connected to a sun roof, bolted to the ground. A sharp stream of light discerned the details. The stand had been blue, but chipped and old paint revealed a brown rusted frame. Her eyes adjusting a little more now, she could see the outline of a young policeman, sitting in the rusted chair, slumped to the right. She could faintly see his eyes- they looked hazy. Drugs? Fatigue? She knew the policemen worked twelve-hour shifts. Something else interrupted her thoughts moving in the darkness- she shifted her gaze downwards. As her eyes moved down, she saw a piece of waggling flesh, up and down up and down, held in the man's hand. It immediately tightened with tension as if her gaze had sparked it awake.

Hagar stepped back in horror.

"Khawaja, pretty khawaja," he murmured again.

And in a moment, just like that, all the tension from the night, that week- reaching back as far as I could remember- pressed on my brain. It pressed hard, flashing. The color of my rage was white. Without time to second guess, without time to let myself think, I lunged at him. With my right hand, I drove a punch into those eyes- those dumb, senseless, hazy eyes. I brought my left knee up, swift, and jammed it into his crotch as hard as I could. For a moment, I was thankful to be wearing those stupid jeans- if only to keep my skin covered from the man's filth.

‏"أنا مصرية ,يا أبن الشرموطه"!

"I am fucking Egyptian, you motherfucking son of a bitch," I hissed back in Arabic.

I ran as fast as I could.

Jesus Time
Cairo

She climbed the last of the stairs, opening a wicker gate that led to the roof of the building. She immediately began scanning for Grace's face. The roof was a wicker-like awning, strung with golden warm Christmas lights. Hiding behind a pair of massive potted plants lining either side of the roof entrance, Hagar's eyes roamed from group to group of middle and high school kids, then up to the stage, around the corner to the right of the entrance. A brief panic settled in when Hagar did not see any sign of Grace anywhere. Would this be the first youth group she attended where nobody she knew was there with her? Should she turn around and leave before someone spotted her? As she considered turning around to leave, she was caught in a tight embrace. She recognized the straw-blonde hair that tickled her face, and when she was finally released, she smiled at Boure. The youth counselor's face always held a mixture of approachable joy and friendliness, her hugs a force of positivity that temporarily overwhelmed anyone being embraced.

"*Girl*, how *are* you today?" Boure said in her high pitched excited voice.

"I am alright. I am here!" Hagar said, shrugging. Boure's eternal cheerfulness always caught Hagar off guard. She usually felt relieved at the wave of cheerfulness, but also felt the need to counterbalance with somber seriousness.

"We are always so filled with joy when you can make it," Boure said, gesturing to the rest of the worship team crowded on the small stage. Hagar forced a smile. "Today's worship will be phenomenal!" she gushed.

Hagar nodded and smiled. She watched as Boure flitted to the next awkward middle schooler who had opened the wicker door, greeting her the same way she greeted Hagar. Hagar walked away, hearing faintly behind her, "Today's worship service will be *phenomenal!*"

Hagar finally spotted Grace around the corner with a group of people. As Hagar approached them, her gaze stopped at Shams. It surprised her he was here this week- his parents had caught him sneaking out of his house last weekend to go drinking, and the rumor was they grounded him. Shams was the son of the pastor at the church- half Egyptian half American, like Hagar. She always imagined this unspoken connection existed between them- the connection of being a half-breed, of being a local but not quite. A magnetic tug and pull between the lost daughter of a mixed faith family and the pastor's son. Standing next to him was Grace, her face animated and her hands waving as she talked to Shams. His attention seemed to be fixed on her, but also fixed at a point beyond Grace- as if he saw her but wasn't really seeing her as she spoke. As Hagar built up the courage to greet Grace, she turned around and, seeing Hagar, rushed to hug her.

"How are ya? Glad you came!" Grace said. Hagar nodded, saying nothing and regaining her somber tone from her earlier interaction with Boure.

"Yeah, shit got weird at home and I almost couldn't make it."

Grace frowned. "Another fight?"

"Yeah. Dad was home."

Grace shook her head. "Well, you're with your church family now. Come over here, we were just talking about the other night when Shams jumped into the Nile on a dare…!"

Grace drug Hagar into the circle. Hagar's gaze rested on

Shams for a second- blushing. Grace noticed and drug Hagar aside, giggling softly.

"I can *feel* you staring at him!" Grace exclaimed.

Hagar blushed. "It's nothing, really," she said defensively.

Grace wrinkled her nose, her soft freckles dancing across her white skin. "Hagar, you can't go for Shams!" she insisted. "He is a mess. Grounded all the time… getting in trouble all the time… He would be a horrible match for a goodie two shoes like you!" Hagar looked inquisitively at Grace. She knew Grace drank on the weekends and snuck out of the house. Lots of kids did it, especially kids from youth group. Hagar never joined them. The thought of asking permission and working out how her father wouldn't find out was just too much to think about. But then again…

"I want to come next time," Hagar blurted, surprised at how much she wanted to go.

Grace's eyebrows raised. "You want to come out with us next time? But how are you going to make that work with your-"

"- I know. Just leave that to me," Hagar said. "I'll make it happen. I'll come out." Hagar's gaze shifted from Grace to Shams.

Grace looked at Hagar sideways, a faint smile on her face. "Okay, but you promise you won't tell? Most of the people we party with- their parents are good for it. But some of them not so much." Grace giggled again and poked Hagar in the side. "Like you, silly! You'll have to be sneaky!"

"I know- like I said, I'll figure it out!" Hagar said, growing irritated with Grace's pokes. She stole a quick glance at Shams, who was combing his curly hair back with one hand and talking animatedly with the other with one of the youth group leaders.

"Alright everyone, let's begin!" A dark-haired young and skinny man with tousled hair announced from the small wooden stage.

"Tonight's worship will be full of the great Word, great songs, and great people!"

Hagar looked to her left and right as everyone took a seat on the ground in front of the stage. He fixated dozens of middle schoolers on him with entranced smiles planted on their faces.

And they sang.

Hagar always loved singing. She knew her voice was not the best- Grace's singing voice would croon velvety notes alongside Hagar's slightly tone-deaf ones. Hagar would settle into a mesmerizing yet alert state of finding minor alto notes to harmonize against the major chords of each song. When she found a harmonizing combination, she would timidly amplify her voice just a little more. It made her feel one with everyone else, but slightly different. Everyone else's voice seemed to almost support hers as it tried to find its sound against every song chorus.

As the singing wound down, they would pass candles around to everyone for opening prayers. The first candle would be lit by the youth pastor leading that evening's sermon, the flame passed around one at a time to each attendee. As girls sat next to their crushes, who were unaware of their presence, Hagar felt the tension between each body of young hormones touching the next. They brushed each other's elbows, softly smiling. Hagar glimpsed Shams sitting on the other side of Grace, who had settled down in between them before the singing had started. He was smiling as Grace turned to him to light his candle. Hagar then tried to make eye contact with him, hoping to receive a smile- or any acknowledgment, really. Instead, he absent-mindedly placed his candle in her general direction, and without looking at her at all continued conversation animatedly with Grace, who was seated on the other side of him.

Everyone was asked to hold hands, leaving their recently lit candles burning in front of them, balancing precariously on their cheap plastic candle holders. Hagar watched Grace reach for Shams' hand out of the corner of her eye. Hagar grasped Shams' other hand, a deep tingle taking over her tactical senses with goosebumps.

"Lord, we pray for each one of your followers here, who only wish to follow in your footsteps as you lead them on the walk their lives hold for them," Boure said.

I would cry during this prayer- most everyone did, but I shed my tears entirely for my predicament. I mourned my inability to pursue a different spiritual path. I mourned my inability to date out of fear. I mourned my lack of independence. That night, I mourned the loss of my damn shorts eaten by the stove's flames. My adolescent mind would think of all the things I could not do and could not have.

Hagar was awakened from her thoughts with a squeeze of her hands by those sitting on either side of her. Tears dried, tissues passed around, shy smiles shared around the circle. All the while she tried to catch Shams' eye, but she failed miserably. Grace had become the star of the show- she always was.

As the service wrapped up for the evening, groups of teenagers were in various stages of getting home before curfew. Hagar rose, looking to say goodbye to Boure. She was nowhere in sight- she must have scurried off to give another enthusiastic hug to another attendee. Hagar turned to find Grace, spotting her by the doorway. Shams was still with her. Hagar bowed her head, staring at her feet for a moment, hoping that maybe when she looked up Shams would be gone. Instead, she saw Shams' hand gently pressed against the small of Grace's back as they descended the staircase to leave.

Hagar started to leave before anyone realized she was standing alone. She made her way slowly, hoping she would miss Grace and Shams on the staircase on the way down. When she opened the door, she saw them below walking side by side, giggling with Shams' hand still resting on Grace's back. Hagar took a deep breath, then headed down the stairs behind them.

Another Horse

Giza, Egypt

Hagar glared at her mother, sitting on the patio at the stables after their pyramids ride. She was hot, hungry, and exhausted. Her mother, however, was in prime spirits. The happiest she had been in a while, Hagar noticed. Lately with the rising amount of fights between her father and mother Hagar noticed her mother was down and gloomy. But today, her mother was excited- she was looking at another horse to buy and take out to the farm, which would finally give her and Hagar a chance to ride out there together since they would have more than one horse.

"Ohhh, Essam, beautiful, beautiful!" the mother crooned as one of the stable hands brought out a beautiful chestnut mare with a blonde mane and tail. The mare was extremely short, Hagar noticed- almost a miniature horse, she thought.

The mother rushed up to the mare, placing a hand on her neck, patting her down. She ran her left hand over the mare's shoulders, towards the withers, tracing the dip back up to the mare's flank. The right hand trailed parallel to the left, tracing the elbow, barrel, then stifle of the horse. The mare cringed in impatience- Hagar couldn't tell if it was the heat, the flies, or the mother's wandering hands that were annoying her the most.

Hagar was in the middle of taking a sip of the sweet mint tea the stable owner had made, happy in her seat. As if she could sense the daughter getting too comfortable, the mother popped her head over the mare's hindquarters, beckoning Hagar over.

"Hagar, come see this mare! She is for you, after all!"

Hagar grimaced. She didn't need or *want* a horse. She was happy with their occasional pyramids ride- she loved seeing the pyramids. But after her last fall on the new stallion they had at the farm, Hagar was skeptical about having her own horse.

"Hagar! Come!" the mother urged. Hagar made a face. "Do I have to?" she whined.

Her mother's face flipped to a stone-faced upset expression, like a light switch. She immediately stopped petting the mare and headed back to her seat on the porch. Hagar could tell she was upset. Hagar rolled her eyes and sighed, then got up to walk towards the horse.

"Okay mom, fine. Yeah, she is great," Hagar said in a monotone, trying to stroke the mare's face. The mare kept throwing her head up and scooting back, clearly not pleased by Hagar's attention. Either that or the flies. In Egypt, one never knew.

The mother ignored Hagar and was in animated conversation with the stable owner. Hagar knew they were haggling the price. She hated those conversations- she always felt uncomfortable, like she didn't belong. Hagar stood awkwardly as the stable hand tried to hold the mare in place. But the mare was getting anxious, and was tired of being told to stand in one spot.

After a few minutes, Hagar saw the mother smile a wide smile and shake hands with the stable owner. They had struck a deal. On a horse for Hagar, that Hagar didn't even want.

The mother took a hasty sip of her sweet mint tea that she had barely touched, then motioned for Hagar to head towards the car. Hagar trotted towards the Jeep in relief. She was eager to get to the breakfast place and was even more excited to get home and shower. She had plans for the evening with Grace and Shams and the crew that she was looking forward to much more than she had horseback riding.

It was silent in the Jeep as the mother and daughter rolled towards the breakfast place. The mother said nothing to the girl- the girl said nothing. Mother was clearly upset about the new mare. But Hagar didn't care- she didn't understand why the mother was pressing horses on her.

You should still be tolerant of this, Hagar. Your mother has been having a hell of a time at home with your father, and it is all because of you...

Trust me, I know. I am completely aware. All the time. It's hard to ignore the yelling in the small ass apartment.

Be grateful, you ungrateful bitch.

The mother parked the Jeep in front of the store and handed Hagar a wad of cash. Without saying a word, Hagar jumped out of the Jeep, scaling the stairs to order their usual order. She waited patiently in the stagnant heat of the store with the flies buzzing lazily around her. When she looked towards the Jeep, the mother was on the phone.

Probably talking to dad or Bakry, telling them the good news that she bought yet another horse... gosh dad is going to be so mad.

The mother's hand waving showed as much. Hagar could see the pallor of the mother's face turn from its usual pale white to red. She must be talking to dad.

Hagar grabbed the sandwiches and headed back to the car once she saw her mother was off the phone. She didn't want to be around the fighting any longer than she needed to be. She hopped in and handed the mother her two sandwiches, and dug into the plastic bag to retrieve her own. They sat in silence in front of the sandwich shop, her mother chewing on the contents of the sandwich in silent contemplation.

"I have something to give you," the mother said.

Hagar looked up at her mother, to see a small cushioned jewelry box in her palm.

"Open it."

Hagar gingerly took the velvety box from her mother and popped the top open. Inside, a small delicate gold necklace sat in a perfect triangle, the pendant the size of Hagar's index finger. A heart with a cross inside it. Hagar looked at her mother in surprise.

"Ma, I love it," Hagar paused, her voice trailing. "But why…?"

"Hagar, you are going through a lot right now. I know you are aware dad and I are fighting a lot," the mother set her sandwich on the dashboard, sighing and put a hand on Hagar's leg. "This is a gift from me to you- a gift to remind you to keep fighting for what *you* think is right, no matter how hard it gets." The mother sighed deeply. "You can't wear it yet," the mother said, closing the box.

"Why? Because dad will see it?" Hagar asked, a slight whine in her voice.

"Dad or anyone else. Wait until you are older and out of the house," the mother said.

"Can I at least wear it on the car ride home?" Hagar asked.

The mother sighed. "Yes, Hagar, you may. This is yours, but I will keep it with me until you are older, maybe in High School, okay?"

Hagar eagerly opened the jewelry box, placing the necklace around her neck and clasping it into place. She smiled. She turned to her mother with an expression of happiness and apprehension. A nagging feeling of annoyance tugged at the corner of Hagar's mind as they drove away from the shop.

If only I could do what I want.

"And mom," Hagar added before her mother started steering into traffic to head home. "Thank you for the horse. I promise I like her."

The mother nodded in satisfaction. Hagar looked out the window, ready for the long ride home.

You lying little bitch.

Swimming in the Nile
Nile Corniche, Cairo

A feeling of thrill crept through Hagar's arms and fingers and heart as she examined the busy Friday night Corniche traffic. She glanced sideways at Grace and Shams, holding hands and giggling at some joke next to her.

Her heart beat faster as she quickly realized that Shams and Grace were drunker than she was. She grabbed at Grace's unoccupied hand with consternation, squeezing her hand firmly to get her friend's attention.

The Corniche was one of the larger speedways in their part of Cairo, with two lanes of traffic going both directions. The road seemed to be in a perpetual state of somewhere between bumper to bumper traffic and just enough room for the small microbuses overloaded with people to speed at hazardous speeds. It was notorious for its pedestrian fatalities. And those were sober locals used to crossing the treacherous street, not drunk young idiots. The longer they waited, the more Hagar's palms sweat. She thought of Deeana- a high schooler who just died trying to cross this very speedway at about the same spot. It was a popular spot for the kids to cross since the felucca docks were dead ahead of them on the other side of the Corniche- but this crossing point was also conveniently at a three way merge with Port Said road- another large artery that led deep into the manicured streets of Al Maadi, a suburb of Cairo. Supposedly, drugs had been involved in that get together that Deeana had attended- that was pretty common for certain circles of the felucca crowd. Nobody was certain. As Hagar watched all the headlights pass, floating in the darkness, it reminded her of all the candles that were lit at the candlelight service for Deeana she had attended with Grace and Shams. The lights floated and bobbed with an eerie feeling echoing of death and crowds of people. More sweat on the palms.

"Grace, focus, we're going to have to cross the street quickly," Hagar said over the car traffic.

Shams glanced over Grace's silky blonde hair waving in the wind, making a face at Hagar.

"Yes MOM!"

Hagar rolled her eyes.

"Yes MOM!" Shams mimicked.

Those types of exchanges had been the full extent of the interaction between Hagar and Shams since him and Grace officially began dating. Since Grace had broken the news, Hagar had only really spent time with Grace when Shams was around.

Hagar saw a gap in traffic coming from their right. She squeezed Grace's hand to signal to go, and the three scurried across the first part of the Corniche, yelling and screaming in the moment's thrill. They scaled the black-and-white checkered sidewalk and stood on the concrete median. `Now, traffic coming from left to right.` Hagar stood on her tiptoes, keeping an eye on traffic, annoyed as Shams' brown wiry hair blew straight up in the wind while he was bent over kissing Grace as she giggled.

`How did I end up the most sober and in charge of this shit?`

She breathed a deep sigh of relief as they reached the black-and-white checkered sidewalk. They stood in front of a green iron gate with Hosni Mubarak's portrait framed at the top. Hagar took a moment to examine his face- he looked young, all of his hair still black, his thin brown eyes looking on unconcerned with the matters of a handful of drunk teenagers gathered below him. Grace had said this was a high school felukkah- as Hagar looked around, she determined the three of them might have been the only Middle Schoolers invited.

Shams stumbled ahead of them and greeted a few of the guys standing in front of the gate. They looked older- maybe even in eleventh or twelfth grade. Shams drug Grace behind him, still holding her hand. Hagar trailed behind.

The felukkah place was a common partying location for high schoolers and middle schoolers alike. Who wouldn't want to rent boats for hours on end and drink while on the Nile? It was the best way for the kids to blend into the darkness of the Nile at night, the silent dark waves cloaks of anonymity while indulging in alcohol, drugs and cigarettes. If the boatmen were cool, make out sessions were an additional indulgence.

Over thirty people were there that night. Word traveled fast. Hagar followed the crowd as everyone moved towards the dock. There were three feluccas strung together side-by-side. When they would take off, all three would in a line. Getting from one boat to the other was as easy as jumping from one to the next.

The kids filed in a line. Hagar hovered behind Grace and Shams. Everyone would have to pay five pounds, a high schooler yelled from the front. A small cheer went up from the crowd- five pounds wasn't bad at all. Hagar stood behind someone she recognized from youth group. The kid was taller with red curly hair. She didn't know his name.

When it was her turn, Hagar stepped forward, paying her five pounds to the boatman standing at the edge of the wooden dock. He looked at her, his glance lingering for a moment.

"انت مصرية؟"

"Are you Egyptian?"

Hagar looked up, startled. How did he know? She usually passed as foreign when with her foreign friends. Panic set in briefly. How should she respond? She had heard of Egyptian students randomly getting arrested for drinking on outings like this- mostly because the Egyptian students insisted on paying local fare, lower than for foreigners. It was technically illegal for Egyptians who were Muslim to drink in Egypt- a rule randomly and erratically enforced. Stories of students coming back from a felucca ride to find policemen waiting for them at the dock were rare but not unusual. The boat hands hated these boat parties thrown by foreigners regardless- but when Egyptian kids were seen at these gatherings, their fury turned to passive aggressiveness.

Hagar smiled, cocking her head to the right, pushing the five-pound note out to him again. "I'm sorry?" she said in English, in the most obnoxious American accent she could muster. "It's five pounds, right?"

The boat hand pursed his lips and shook his head, taking her five-pound note and pressing it into the rest.

The extra time it had taken to pay her entry fee separated Hagar from Grace and Shams. She didn't know anyone here. Hagar looked around desperately. She located them on the farthest boat from the dock, fishing around a cooler for more alcohol. Hagar hopped from the dock to the first boat, then the first boat to the second. Hagar found an unopened Sakkara beer that looked like it was just taken out of a cooler, sitting on the front of the felucca as she was passing. She looked around her to see if anyone was watching, then grabbed the bottle. She popped the top open with her sweater cuff over her hand and settled down next to Grace, who was engaged in a lively conversation with another one of Shams' acquaintances.

`Everyone knew Shams.`

With no one to talk to, Hagar turned around and observed the Nile at night as the feluccas moved away from the shore. There was enough sunlight left lingering in the sky for her to almost count emerald ripples in the Nile as other boats floated by. Flickers of gold shone on the waves, reflections of warm lights coming from the tall skyscrapers and hotels on the shore. The small flitting pieces of gold crawled across the dark waves like glittering gold worms weaving through the night.

Elevated voices right next to her on the boat broke her daze. Hagar peered over Grace's shoulder- it was Shams. He was standing by the mast with two other guys. All had beers in their hands, talking animatedly, waving their arms. Hagar peered a little closer trying to see what they were gesturing at- before she knew it, Shams was jumping into the water.

Is this a stunt he does every time?

The two high schoolers who were standing by him started cheering. Shams disappeared. Grace quickly set her beer down on the table in front of her and leaned over the side of the boat.

"I can't see him!" she screeched. "Where did he go?"

Hagar looked back to the man at the back manning the felucca, steering it along with his two other colleagues on the adjoined boats. He was motioning to the other two boatmen to stop and throw down their anchors. Hagar could hear him clearly over the din.

"ياسطا !واحد منهم دخل في المياه !هو أجنبي بس مش متأكد"!

"Hey! A guy overboard! I think he is white but not sure!" The felucca hand yelled.

"هات أحمد هنا حالا"!

"Get Ahmed over here *now*!"

Hagar watched as the boatman on the middle boat leaped to the boat on the far left to fetch Ahmed. His steps were nimble despite the number of drunk people in his way. He leapt from the pointy front of the felucca, one to the other, using the mast as the way to balance, his legs stretched. As he reached the third boat, one of the high schoolers pointed towards the dark.

The young boatman, Ahmed, presumably, followed his pointed finger. Hagar sat up further on the back platform of the boat to get a look. She could see a mop of curly hair rise to the surface. One of Shams' arms shot up with a hang loose sign, and people from all three boats cheered. Hagar did not cheer, but listened to the boatman next to her grumble to the second boatman watching the action.

"ابن المتناكة ان شاء الله يجيله بلهارسيا بعد الحركة دي !هو مش عارف ايه اللي في النيل؟! وساخة"!

"Son of a bitch- I hope he gets bilharzia. Doesn't he know what is in the Nile? Filth!"

"المفروض نتصل بالبوليس ـنطلعه من شعرنا و نخلص منه"!

"We should call the police. Get him out of our hair for good."

"مش مع كل الأجانب هنا يا عم .أحسن نرجع دلوقتي و نأخذ البقشيش علي طول و نخلص من البهاوي .أكره حفلات ذي دول"!

"Not with this many white people here, man. Let's just try to turn back home and get our tips as soon as possible and see these idiots away. I hate parties like this."

"أنا معاك يا عمو .يمكن ابن الكلب يجيله البلهارسيا بس احتمال أحنا بعيد عن الشاطئ … ميستحقش يموت موت عبد الحليم كده ولا كده"…

"I agree, man. Maybe the kid will get bilharzia, but I don't think we are close enough to shore for him to get it. "

The boatmen sat side by side, crouched with their *galabiyas* pulled up around their waists. Ahmed the boatman and the two high schoolers pulled Shams back on board. The second boatman went back to his perch on the second boat, and in unspoken agreement all three boatmen lifted their anchors and turned the boats around to head back to the dock. Hagar remained sitting on the back platform near the boatman manning the oar of their felucca. She watched Grace scuttle over to Shams, hugging him in drunken tears, scolding him for scaring the shit out of her, etc, etc.

Hagar stared down at her now empty beer bottle, and the hum of the three boats silenced a bit more than everyone realized the boats were turning back around. Against the wind, Hagar could hear their boatman humming and singing under his breath- lost to anyone except those quiet enough to listen. She smiled as she recognized the tune, an old familiar Abd El Halim song her father used to sing to her and Bakry when they were younger-

"أهواك...

اهواك و اتمنى لو انساك...

و انسى روحى وياك...

وان ضاعت يبقى فداك لو تنسانى"

"I love you

I love you, and I wish I could forget you

And forget my soul with you

And if it gets lost, then it remains yours if you ever forget me..."

The Mosque
Giza

"*Yalla ya ayal*[8] it is time to go!" the father called.

Bakry's footsteps pounded down the hallway. He was excited to go to the mosque today to show off the new *galabiyya* the father bought for him. It came straight from Makkah in the father's suitcase from his *hajj* trip. Bakry's excitement made Hagar roll her eyes, laying her head down on her notebook. She still had plenty of homework to do. The studying was a good way to keep her mind off of the inevitable mosque trip that evening, and from plotting how to get to the party that night. It was Thursday night- the night everyone went out. Grace had called a few hours earlier and invited Hagar to some high school house party- but it's not like she would have gone, anyway. Her mother would have never allowed her to attend any type of party, even under the guise of spending the night at Grace's house. Part of her was happy at turning down Grace's invitation- she couldn't imagine having to be the third wheel to the Grace-and-Shams show. "No, sorry, I have plans," Hagar recalled herself saying. Besides, it was Thursday night. And Thursday nights were for going to the mosque in the Khalifa household.

"Hagar, please get going and please- put proper clothes on," the father said, throwing a look full of judgment at the sight of

---

[8] Arabic for "God is good," usually said in response to seeing something good and something to be thankful for."

her bare calves. Did he look under my desk to see what I was wearing? How does he *do* that? "This is not proper for the mosque."

"Baba!" she said as firmly as she could, turning around in her seat. "These are not shorts. They are capris. The only part of my legs showing are my calves and ankles." She knew his response, but was so irritated at the thought of going to the mosque she knew it would aggravate her father.

"Hagar, wear a hijab and cover your hair when you go to the mosque," he said, grabbing her shoulders from behind. "Not showing any part of your legs! Now, come on. I don't want a hard time like last time. You *will* go today, even if I have to carry you to the car myself."

The mother appeared in Hagar's bedroom doorway. "Hagar, how are you doing on homework?" she asked.

"*You will not do this!*" the father roared, turning to the mother, with one hand still on Hagar's shoulder. "GO!" He said to Hagar, shoving her towards her closet, prompting her to find something proper to wear.

The mother and Hagar looked at one another briefly. *I tried,* her mother's eyes said as she backed away from the doorway. Hagar turned to face her closet, searching for her Levi's and black shirt.

Hagar's father attended a large mosque near the pyramids. She had never attended the mosque until she transferred to her new school- a bargain between her parents in moving schools. Every week, every Thursday night Hagar would attend the mosque. Many fights had ensued over the topic, her mother resisting the idea of Hagar attending the mosque as a young girl in an environment full of men. Night after night the parents fought, with Hagar listening intently through the walls between her bedroom and theirs. "She is my daughter- she is a Muslim! She must learn her religion and practice it every day!" During those fights, every night would end with the mother coming into

Hagar's bedroom, rubbing Hagar's back until she slept as the girl cried over the prospect of having to go to the mosque. Her father, irritated with the whole family at that point, would slam doors and leave the apartment, leaving the three of them to spend another night without him.

Hagar would listen, wondering why her mother tolerated her father's constant nagging about their daughter's daily dose of religion when he was hardly home. The days he was not home were peaceful, and when he visited, it was only for a couple of hours in the evening. He never stayed the night. Occasionally, he would even forget the mosque nights, forgetting to pick up Hagar and Bakry (to Hagar's relief and Bakry's disappointment). As she listened to the strained whispers continue in the hall, Hagar tried to recall the last time her father and mother slept in the same bedroom. `Who cares if it's not normal. It's so quiet when he is not here.`

Hagar finished changing clothes. She was in her usual Levi's jeans and a long-sleeved black shirt that made her sweat in the summer heat. Her mother wrapped Hagar's blonde curls in a red bandana. Her father glanced at her as she walked into the dining room, wrinkling his nose.

"Is there nothing else she can wear?" he asked the mother, looking at his daughter with his eyebrows drawn together in disapproval.

The mother crossed her arms, shaking her head. "You wanted her covered, here she is."

And so off they went.

As they drove on the Corniche, Hagar gazed into the Nile's dull reflection. Her thoughts wandered back to Grace and Shams. They were probably watching a movie, or pre-gaming before the party started. Hagar thought of the other Egyptian girls at the American school who came from Muslim families. They never went to the mosque, ever. When she asked her father why this was the case, he would look at her with pride and say,

"Because you are *my* daughter and in our family it is tradition to go to the mosque every week, at least. The Khalifa family traces directly back to the Prophet, and we must never forget this." He would pause dramatically. "Remember, Hagar, you are -"

"-A Khalifa," Hagar said, rolling her eyes. This made her father grin from ear to ear.

She would feel the strongest anger she ever felt making the drive to the mosque- the low, burning urge to scream at her father, telling him to leave her alone, to let her be.

Wasn't two religion lessons a week enough? What if I didn't feel like being the Muslim girl he wanted me to be?

They would always drive by the Pyramids, past Ramses square to reach the mosque. Unlike the drive to the farm in the early mornings, Thursday night drives would always be heavy with traffic the moment they exited the Ring Road to Giza. If she was lucky, she would get a few minutes to examine the pyramids from afar. They passed the winding side street that led to the horse stables. For a second, she was horseback on a rolling desert hill, looking back on Giza and see the sprawling city. Her mother was by her side, comfortable in their silence.

Every time they arrived at the mosque, Hagar would notice that no other girls her age were there. She was the youngest seated in the cramped women's section upstairs, too short to reach the gaps through the *mashrabiyya* to glimpse the Sheikh during the sermon. She would absorb stares from the men milling in the prayer area, who would make their way across the prayer floor to greet Hagar's father as soon as they spotted the family. Hagar would keep her head down, her eyes on the intricate geometry of the carpets under her feet. Bakry craved their attention, telling them stories about religion class and his extra tutoring lessons. The sheikh was both Hagar and Bakry's religion tutor, and Bakry would run into his arms and soon be engulfed by the black and gold-lined folds of the Sheikh's flowing robes. The sheikh ruffled Bakry's coarse curls. Men at the mosque paid little attention to Bakry, instead approaching Hagar and ask about her American school. Did it have a uniform? No? Then what would govern what the students could and couldn't wear? No religion lessons? But she was still taking Arabic classes- good, good. She would cling to her father's side, silent, wishing they would leave her alone.

She hated taking her shoes off at the entrance of the mosque. When finally seated upstairs, the women would always joke that for every pair of shoes they "lost" at the mosque for Thursday night prayer, the more *hasanat* or rewards they would receive in God's book of good deeds. Hagar would mumble about just wanting her shoes back, tired of the constant theft at the doors of mosques. Some women's noses would wrinkle with disapproval, stating that if the poor were stealing shoes, they must need them more than they did. Other women would snicker in agreement, shaking their heads at the injustice.

Hagar would trace the geometric cut-outs of the *mashrabiyya* during the sermon as she tried to pay attention. She could feel herself nod, a mixture between exhaustion and boredom eventually leading to sleep. The women would always be ready to catch her, cradling her head of golden curls in her lap. Hagar slept lightly and every once in a while as her consciousness floated in and out, she could hear the women would quietly scuffle about her, stroking each ringlet of her hair, marveling at how smooth the girl's curls were. On some visits, her father would make her attend the sermon downstairs with the men. Hagar would keep her head down, and slouched as if to disappear from view, feeling the men's glazed stares around her boring holes into her skin. She never slept through sermons when she was downstairs, her unease and discomfort keeping her awake. One woman once asked her why her father would make her worship downstairs, stating it was improper for a woman to sit amongst men during time of worship.

"He is a partial owner of the mosque, he does what he pleases! He is the doctor!" And the conversation would stop there.

Hagar never understood what this meant, until one Thursday night, her father showed her and Bakry the basement of the mosque. The sermons usually ended very late at night, close to nine or ten. Then it would be an hour drive back to their apartment. That night after the sermon, Hagar's father pulled her and Bakry aside after they had put their shoes on outside the prayer room door that led to the street..

"*Ayal*, I want to show you something," he said.

Hagar sighed. "Baba, it's very late. And we still need to drive home."

Her father gave her a stern look. His thick and long eyebrows dropped, unfurling to almost entirely cover his dark eyes. The father's forehead, slick with sweat, the loose folds of skin lined with droplets of moisture, deepened with a frown. His lips would press together in a frustrated pout, poking out from his mustache and beard.

"Hagar, you *will* come," he said, taking a hold of her hand. It was not rough- he had a way of engulfing her small hand in his large brown paw, firmly pulling her in the direction he wished to go.

The mosque was very large. Hagar always avoided the back hallways and stairways, she would become disoriented in a matter of seconds, usually searching for the bathroom. Down one of these hallways and two flights of stairs they went. At the bottom of the staircase, Hagar found herself in a library. An oriental rug of dark burnt red hues was in front of her, with two identical heavy wooden tables on either side of it. Bookshelves lined the walls behind the tables. Past the bookshelf to her right, an oval doorway led to another room, where she could glimpse more bookcases. At the far end of the small room they had entered was a very large Quran open on a wooden reading stand. This was the first thing that captured her attention, and she ran towards it. It had to be at least half of her body height, the scripture letters as big as one of her hands. She flipped pages, admiring the large text. So engrossed with the enormous book, she almost missed her father saying:

"This is your grandfather's library. These are his books. They named it in his honor."

Bakry was examining the spines of the books lining the left side of the room, running his fingers over the gold lettering.

"Baba, Grandfather came to this mosque?" Bakry asked.

"Your grandfather helped build this mosque," the father said. "He was the founder."

Hagar glimpsed up from the large Quran. She saw her father gently take Bakry's hand and led the boy to a shelf. The father picked a book and walked to the closest chair- a rickety plastic fold out chair awkwardly placed next to the bookshelf. He handed the book to Bakry gently, then lifted him onto his lap. Bakry's slight frame for his age almost appeared to sink into the large one of his fathers'. Bakry smiled widely, his gaze focused on his father's face. His father looked back at him tenderly, whispering to him in Arabic. The boy opened the book and read the words quietly to his father.

The more Bakry read, the more dad's figure slouched over Bakry's slight frame, as if about to engulf him into his embrace. They were quiet and happy. I suddenly felt far away. Like I wasn't there at all.

Enough Love for Two?
Cairo, High School years

Hagar was relieved when she received an invitation for a girls-only sleepover from Grace. It had been two years since she and Shams had dated, and Hagar couldn't remember the last time they had spent time together alone, let alone a girl's sleepover night.

Hagar slung her overnight bag from one shoulder to the next on the way to Grace's house. Her spirits were low, but she knew they'd improve once she arrived. Now that she was in high school, the visits to the mosque had slowed down. Tonight, her father arrived at home right as Hagar was leaving. He went into a roaring rage when he discovered Hagar was going to Grace's for a sleepover. Hagar had been forced to stay home every week for weeks now just in case her father came to take her to the mosque. This seemed all too ironic and coincidental that he showed up the one night she HAD made plans. Her mother had blessed off on the sleepover- Hagar had left the two fighting and yelling at the top of their lungs, with Bakry waiting forlorn in the dining room with his galabeyya on, ready to go. Hagar knew he had felt abandoned the past few weeks when their father had not shown up- there is no way the mother would allow him to go to the mosque on his own, with him still being in middle school. Bakry gave Hagar a look of deep hatred in passing as she left the house with her overnight bag. She stuck out her tongue in response. Stupid little boy.

Hagar internalized the fight as she walked to Grace's. Grace was used to hearing about the fights- probably fed up. Grace cut Hagar's complaints short, telling Hagar it was normal, and would quickly change the subject. Hagar had noticed Boure and some of the other people at the youth group had been doing the same. Everyone has gotten tired. It's old news to them.

Well, can you blame them? It's old news to you.

They could just listen. I'm not asking them to solve it. Although that *would* be nice.

But to them, this is a problem you have to live with. Cope with. It is not something solvable.

So I am supposed to live with this for the rest of my life?

Possibly, yes.

Bullshit. I'll run away from home before that has to happen.

But you can never leave them behind…

I certainly can. I will certainly try.

Hagar forcibly silenced my voice in her head as she scaled the stairs to Grace's apartment. Once let in, Hagar headed straight for Grace's bedroom where she found Grace folding her clothes.

Hagar's attempts at appearing upbeat didn't quite work. On seeing Hagar's face when she came into Grace's room, Grace immediately asked her what had happened.

Just another fight.

Hagar expected the conversation to end at that. But Grace unexpectedly kept going..

"Why doesn't your mother just… leave him?" Grace asked suddenly.

"Leave who? My father?" Hagar said, incredulous.

"Yeah. Like- why doesn't she just leave your dad?"

Because she is a Christian woman married to a Muslim man. Because she would lose all rights to her children if she did that. Because she would likely have to leave the country. Because you and Bakry are underage, so you automatically belong to father since he is the only Muslim in the marriage.

Hagar was silent in response to Grace's question, and Grace continued-

"Well, maybe she doesn't want to leave. Maybe she still stays because she thinks your dad will get better but really he is worse than she knows."

Hagar raised an eyebrow at the last sentence. Worse than she knows?

"Worse than she knows?" Hagar echoed out loud. "What do you mean by that?"

Hagar sat on the edge of her bed with her overnight bag on the ground. Grace began wringing one shirt she was about to fold. Fidgeting was uncharacteristic.

"Well... you know Zein, right?" Grace asked nervously.

"Zein... Shams' best friend?" Hagar asked tersely. "Of course. What's going on?" What did Shams have to do with my family? Could they not go a single night without mentioning his name?

"Well... he told me something very disturbing today," Grace said, her voice uncertain and slow. "I don't know if now is a good time to tell you," she said.

"Just say it, Grace," Hagar said, exasperated. She slid down from on top of Grace's bed to sitting on the ground, slumping her back against the bed frame. How could this get any worse? And now do I have to sit here and listen to more stories about Shams?

"Hagar, your father has another family," Grace blurted, stumbling over her words. She had stopped wringing the shirt, and slumped next to Hagar at the foot of the bed, leaning her back against the bed next to her.

"Your father has another wife."

Hagar stared at Grace, with no change in expression.

"How do you know?" Hagar finally asked.

Grace paused, staring at the white cami in her hands. "Zein's aunt was at his house earlier this week. Him, Shams and I were hanging out at Zein's house," Grace's words stumbled out as she struggled to fill.

Hagar grimaced. It hurt more to hear about Grace talking about hanging out with Shams than the news about my father. And it had been two years already.

"Anyway, his aunt walked in with his mom… Zein's mom, that is… his aunt mentioned her husband- and said your dad's name." Grace looked up and Hagar, uneasily. "At first I thought I heard wrong…"

"Huh. If all of this is right, then Zein and I are related.. That is crazy!"

No, it couldn't be right, none of it.

"Are you serious?" Grace's voice was deadpan.

"What do you mean am I serious? That would mean that me and Shams' best friend… are *related*! That is insane!"

She wondered if Shams knew… he must know. Maybe that would be a subject of conversation between them at some point?

No, you idiot, likely a subject of extreme shame. Your mother is married to a man with two wives.

Grace shook her head, her freckled face flushed.

"Hagar, your dad has a second wife! That is fucking insane!"

Hagar looked down at her hands as the news sank in.

"Well, Grace, what the fuck am I supposed to do?" then, without thinking; "Wait… Shams knows about this?"

"Hagar, it's bad enough…! And- yes of course Shams knows, he was *there*! Why does that matter?" Grace exclaimed, confused.

"Hagar, it's not right- your mom being married to him. Don't tell me you haven't thought it might be better if they divorced,"

Grace urged. "If they get the divorce, you could be whoever you want! You could go to church! You could date boys! Go to parties! Hell, you could even go to college in the States without figuring out how to sneak around him! This is the perfect reason for your mom to leave him!"

Hagar sat up slowly, confused. I knew it wasn't uncommon for Muslim men to have many wives. But I knew no man- from my old school, from the mosque, from anywhere- who had more than one wife. I had learned from religion lessons that this phenomenon only existed in a few approved conditions set by the prophet long ago. My teachers had presented it as an anomaly, as something that rarely happened, and mostly happened amongst poorer families. If a man's brother died, he would take on his brother's wife to provide for her. Stuff like that.

But not my father.

And not my family.

This stuff happened in other families, not mine.

Hagar came to when she heard Grace ask:

"Hagar, will you tell your mother?"

Hagar rose from the ground, grabbing her overnight bag. "I have to go," Hagar said abruptly, heading for the door, her overnight bag slung over one shoulder.

The Most Awkward of Dinners
Cairo

Hagar stormed back home in a rage. Her mind replayed all the fights they had had- imagining how angry her father would be at her mother, how her mother's face would turn red with rage then white after he hit her. And he had another wife?!

Did he hit her too?

Of course he does- he is an Egyptian man. What Egyptian man doesn't hit his wife?

Does he fight with her like he does with mom?

Probably not- sounds like she is probably a good Muslim wife who obeys her husband.

Why did he need another wife? Why did he need mom?

Greed?

Thrown into a new fit of silent rage at my last response, Hagar raced up the stairs once she got to her apartment building. Before she did, she glanced across the street- the basket cart was mysteriously gone. Everything suddenly felt wrong- felt off.

Hagar fiddled with her keys, trying to unlock the front door. She was shaking too hard to do it, and before she knew it her father had opened the door and was staring at her in surprise.

"What happened to the sleepover?"

Hagar pushed past him, turning left into the dining room. She halted as if surprised to see Bakry and her mother sitting at the table. They were in the middle of eating dinner.

The mother could see something was terribly wrong and rose quickly, walking towards Hagar. She grabbed Hagar by the arm, trying to lead her towards her room. Hagar stood her ground.

"No, you all need to hear this," Hagar said, her voice low with anger.

Her mother's grip tightened on Hagar's arm. "Hagar, I am sure whatever is going on we can talk about in your room. Your father and Bakry are eating dinner." Hagar could tell her mother was not up for another fight.

Hagar jerked her arm away from her mother's grip, motioning for her to sit down at the table. The mother gave Hagar a stern look, bracing for the worst as she sat down.

"Bakry, go get Hagar some food. Make her a plate," the father commanded. Bakry whined- father's no-nonsense look sent Bakry flying to the kitchen.

"I… I just can't believe it," Hagar said, shaking as she stood in the same spot.

"Hagar, what the hell is wrong? We have had enough of an evening as it is. Why aren't you at Grace's house?" the mother demanded. The father stared at his plate and continued to shovel food in his mouth, completely disregarding his daughter. Hagar's face turned hotter.

"He… HE HAS ANOTHER ONE!" Hagar said, pointing at her father. "He- he- has another *wife*! And we had… no idea!"

Hagar's mother immediately put her head in between her hands. Hagar's eyebrows went up with surprise. I don't know what I was expecting her to do- but not that.

Hagar heard a clatter and clash behind her. The family turned to see Bakry, holding a glass of water in one hand. He held his disfigured hand in front of him, his face filled with surprise. A broken plate spewed the dinner of mashed potatoes, a slice of meat and green beans all over the floor. Bakry's mouth hung open. He clearly heard Hagar- there was no way anyone in the house couldn't hear her.

"Bakry, Goddamnit!" the mother yelled. "Why didn't you carry the plate of food in your good hand? For the love of God, how many times have we been over this?" The mother rushed over to where Bakry was standing, pushing him aside to examine the food on the floor. "What are you waiting for?" she barked, "Go get the rubbish bin and rags! Clean this mess up!" The mother stood up and rushed into the kitchen, as if she had yelled those instructions to herself more than she had to Bakry. Bakry looked on at Hagar's face, confused, then broke eye contact to look back into the kitchen. He came to his senses and ran in. Hagar watched after the mother.

I can't fucking believe it. She hears the news and runs into the kitchen?! No response? Nothing!

Hagar turned back to her father. He was sitting at the table, his fork and knife clutched in his brown bear hands. His eyes looked at her, but they said nothing. His face was blank. Hagar looked at him incredulously, expecting some type of answer. Even anger would be acceptable at this point- anything to allow Hagar to yell and scream at the top of her lungs. He had betrayed her- betrayed the family. And yet he still sat there, fat and sweaty, entitled to his meal?

Hagar could hear the mother scolding Bakry in the kitchen. Both were still in there. Why didn't they come out? How long would I have to wait for a response?

And there she stood, completely silent, still shaking with rage.

It finally hit me that nobody was coming out of the kitchen. Soon I heard small sobs. My father said nothing as he ate his dinner, ignoring my presence. And mother wouldn't come out, preoccupied with taking care of Bakry. The hurt- swelling outrage, the feeling that what was happening was not right- swelled up inside me.

"Fucking fine, everyone! *Fine!* Let's all ignore it and pretend like it didn't happen!"

Hagar waved her overnight bag in the air with one hand. She directed her voice at the still statue that was her father, sitting at the dinner table. She turned on her heel, stomped to her room, slammed the door shut, and burst into a tearful heap onto her bed.

***

It was not until years later that I had discovered my father had lied too. When I confronted him later about his second wife, he had claimed she was dead after a sickness. Then, in my Facebook feed, I saw a photo.

"Mom w Baba fe el beit," it said. "Mom and dad at home."

I remember stopping at the photo, with no emotion at first. Her face, or the colorful scarf she wore as a hijab, or how short she must have been standing by father did not fixate me. I studied the heavy wooden door behind them, the marble floor they were standing on, and the colorful painting in the background. A nice light fixture hung behind them.

And the thing I could feel was the burning jealousy at how their family had perfect marble floors and nice light fixtures in their house, and we did not.

***

Hagar sat for the last few steps of the trot as they slowed

down. They rode on a newly dug road, the soft sand pushed to the sides to create a somewhat even ground for cars to drive over. Hagar squinted in the sunlight to get a better look of what was ahead.

Her and the mother were riding the two horses at the farm over the new road the father had boasted of digging the day before. The mother thought it would be a good reason to ride the horses out. The father had impulsively bought more land, expanding the farm just a few weeks prior. Hagar had wondered about this decision after hearing a few whispered conversations about how the farm was not making the family any money yet, and was barely paying for itself. The mother and father were clearly worried, but continued to push forward with expanding their project. Hagar remembered shaking her head as she had paused in front of the bedroom door, their worried whispers carrying in the quiet apartment.

Her mother and father had not spoken to her or Bakry about the night Hagar came home from Grace's house. It had been a few weeks since then- the father barely came home after that night, when he had finished his dinner and simply left the house without a word. The mother had not addressed the matter directly with Hagar at all, continuing on the family's existence as if nothing had happened. Hagar had withstood it playing the silent, quiet game. But she was fed up. This was almost worse than the constant fighting- now silence weighed heavy with avoided confrontations. Whenever Hagar had asked to go out or to Grace's house, the mother let her go. She had spent no time with Hagar until today, when the mother had proposed (commanded) the girl to go on a ride to see the new land father bought.

They both came to a stop at a pine treeline that marked the border of their land. The new parcel was right ahead of them. It was just a vast amount of desert. Hagar could see another line of pine trees in the distance-presumably someone else's land started there. The new parcel was one large rolling hill, covered in rocks and pebbles. Unlike the west side of their property, the land to the east donned a rocky crust- the surface of a candy bar covered with nuts. Hagar knew father bought the land to drill for water there- it was too far away from the old well. Soon the land would be red-gold, enriched by the water that would be pumped from the Libyan Watershed that flowed beneath the Egyptian Western desert.

They stood in silence, the lack of words humming and swirling between them, intermingled with the desert air. Hagar knew the mother could stand there for hours without saying a thing, but the young girl's mind wouldn't stop anxiously coming close to bubbling over, aching to talk about the other night.

"Mom-" Hagar said suddenly. Her mare shifted, anxious about standing still in the wind.

The mother remained stone-faced and quiet, not responding. Hagar continued.

"Mom, I have to ask. Did you know? About dad's other wife?"

The mother looked down at her hands and exhaled.

"Yes, Hagar, I knew."

Hagar's heart dropped.

"When?" she asked, her voice shaking. Did I really want to know the answer to that?

"Before I married him." She said it as if confessing a deepest sin, quietly, softly, hesitantly.

"Hagar, I was pregnant with you. I had no choice. I had to. You will understand when you are older- life is not always that simple with these decisions."

"But mom, how?" Hagar pressed.

"Hagar, you know the law is not on my side as a Christian foreign woman marrying your father. If I had not married him,

I would have lost you forever."

Hagar frowned. "Only if you had stayed in Egypt. You could have gone back to America and had me there, and everything would have been fine!" Hagar felt a moment of longing at the idea of being raised in the States by just her mother, without Bakry and her father there. It felt right. It would have felt right, she thought.

"Hagar, raising a baby alone is not as easy as you think," she said in a scolding tone. "Now, enough of this. You know why now. I don't want you to bring it up again. I don't want you to bring it up in front of Bakry either- you know how he idolizes his father, and hearing the news the other night the way you did it- it was horrible to him."

Her tone was almost accusatory. Hagar felt a flash of anger bubble up again. Mother was concerned about how Bakry took the news? How badly he had reacted? How about *me*? *My* feelings? *My* thoughts around it? The feelings of complete betrayal? How I had stayed up that night, piecing everything together? No wonder dad was gone- he lived somewhere else. Another home. Another woman. Who knows- even other kids!

"Hagar, promise me," the mother's stern voice interrupted her thoughts.

"Okay, mom," Hagar said flatly. There was no point pressing the subject. Her mother was clearly not in the mood to hear Hagar talk about how she felt.

You're just going to suck it up. Just like you do everything else.

I am so angry... This is not fair.

This is not the first time you have had to do this. We know how to do this well.

The mother turned her stallion to the right, taking another newly made road back towards the house. The road was soft, cushiony sand. Hagar paused, holding the mare in place before pulling in the reins and following the mother.

There was a slight swelling in her throat, as if something was caught there, fighting to come out, and all Hagar could do was swallow, again and again, trying to push it down.

Part III: Zakat Almsgiving)

Rave

Sakkara Pyramids

Hagar opened her room door and looked out into the hallway. It seemed everyone was asleep, but she wanted to make sure. She looked down and checked on her outfit before she began the walk towards the front door. With her breasts blooming shortly after starting her period, she felt a burst of pride and the heat of shame at the same time as she looked down at the t-shirt she was wearing. It was a hand-me-down from Grace- a deep black V-neck t-shirt. On Grace it hadn't looked the slightest bit provocative- but on Hagar, it made her feel like the women in the magazines and the movies. Attractive? Hot? Definitely not beautiful.

She looked up again and re-assessed the hallway. Ok, nobody is awake. Hagar timidly stepped out, aware of all the spots where the loose tiles creaked. She hopped from one tile to the next- all the silent ones- as carefully as she could. She finally reached the front door, gently turning the door handle. She stepped outside and eased the door closed. It had a proclivity for slamming and it was hard to resist the heavy wood as it fought to slam closed.

She ran outside and hailed a cab. She would pick up Grace, then they would cab all the way to the Sakkara pyramids. The entire plan was insane. She thought of Grace's tear-drenched face, insisting on going to the rave the night before. She knew going was a bad idea- but after Grace and Shams' breakup; it seemed like Grace needed to pretend like things were normal.

Yes, Grace and Shams had broken up. Hagar was misty on the exact details, but knew it had something to do with Shams going out without Grace one weekend, getting in trouble then getting grounded. Grace had believed she and Shams had made progress reigning in his drinking and sneaking out of the house even on weekdays to go out with the high school guys. But... apparently not. Shams was still attending youth group on Wednesdays- Hagar figured his father didn't consider youth group a social activity. Grounding Shams from going out and hanging out with friends was one thing- but church and youth group were essential activities. Maybe Shams' parents figure the youth counselors will fix him, Hagar mused.

As the cab arrived in front of Grace's apartment, Hagar saw shimmers of glitter in the darkness. Soon, Grace appeared and hopped into the back next to Hagar. Hagar's eyebrows raised in surprise at Grace's outfit- a deep cut blouse covered in glittery sequins and tight jeans. Hagar blushed as Grace flounced into the taxi, catching the taxi driver's ogling eyes.

"Hellooo!" Grace said, full of excitement and energy. She turned to the taxi driver, giving him the location. He raised his eyebrows and said something in Arabic about the location being very far away. Grace looked at Hagar questioningly she didn't understand Arabic. Hagar leaned forward and for a few minutes bargained with the taxi driver. Hagar offered to pay for half of the cost of the taxi driver to make it back to their side of town from Giza province- they finally agreed on a price and the taxi driver headed towards the Corniche.

"So- we are going to a rave?" Hagar asked Grace. She already knew the answer, but was still astonished at the choice of activity. She was wrestling with this deep, uneasy feeling going so far to an outing that included primarily drug use amongst other things- Hagar just didn't feel comfortable with it.

"Yeah, Hagar, a rave," Grace said, exasperated. "I told you- I will not do any drugs, they'll have alcohol there if you want to drink," Grace smirked. "I'm DEFINITELY drinking tonight!"

"Okay," Hagar said, hesitating "It's just still fucking weird you chose a rave of all things. It's usually just- drinking somewhere."

"Yeah, well, I feel like changing it up," Grace said, lifting her chin up in defiance. "Just because Shams & I broke up doesn't mean I should stop going out."

"What do you mean?" Hagar asked.

"Well, we are going to go meet his friends there," Grace said, her voice tinged with guilt. Hagar looked at her and shook her head.

"So, Shams might be there is what you're saying?" Hagar asked.

"Well, yeah…" Grace's voice wandered as she opened her purse and began rummaging. She located some lip gloss, pulling the goopy wand out and applying it, using the taxi driver's rear-view mirror. Hagar glared at the taxi driver as he watched Grace's every move with the same stare as before.

Put your dick back in your pants, idiot.

"Ok, let's just… try to have a good time ok?" Hagar said, glancing back at Grace as she put the lip gloss back in her purse. "No drama, no drinking too much, no crying- let's just have a good time. We both deserve it."

"Yeah, yeah, of course girl!" Grace quipped back in a cheerful voice. "I just want to go out, you know. Nothing crazy, no drama."

The drive to the Sakkara pyramids area was familiar to Hagar, taking much of the same route from the East side of Cairo and the Nile to the West. Driving the 6th of October bridge reminded her of the farm. The Nile was darker at night, almost indiscernible from the Western shores where the few plots of farmland remain unlit at night, resting in the arms of the dark and vaguely emerald waves of the river. But the lights, when they were present, were brighter at night with an almost aggressive festivity to them. Festively lit boats crowded the river immediately under the bridge as families and young people sang at the top of their lungs to popular Arabic songs, drinking sweet black tea with the occasional shisha pipe here and there. Each boat seemed to compete with the next on the extent of elaborate Christmas light decorations they could fit on the boat's awning. Some lights would flash erratically with no rhyme or reason- others would sparkle to music. Gardens of flowers formed by the stringed lights covered the boat's awnings with the occasional pair of dolphins leaping towards one another at the front or back of the boat. Others illustrated scenes from the pyramids and the Sphinx, mixed yet with Quranic verses or God's name (Allah) strung skillfully in calligraphy. Hagar stared out of the window of the taxi in silence, feeling completely powerless as the lights assaulted her vision left and right below. Occasionally her view was blocked by flocks of families fishing off of the sides of the bridge. Intermittently both sides of the bridge would crowd groups of wicker chairs and tables for those fishing to sit and take a break. Hagar scoffed at the vendors that hovered on either side of the road, blocking a whole lane of traffic. Most of them were makeshift donkey carts or hand-pulled carts, each selling their own delicious snack to hungry fishing expeditions. Hagar watched as the taxi rolled by each tasty snack slowly; fire roasted corn on the cob; *arq esous*, a sweet licorice drink made by soaking licorice roots in water with molasses or honey served in a plastic bag with a straw; roasted peanuts, chickpeas soaked in lemon water (*termous*), fire-roasted sweet potato (*batata*) and homemade potato chips fried right there in front of hungry late night weekenders.

As the scenes of Nile-goers faded and the ill-lit red-brick of the slums came to view, Hagar redirected her attention back to Grace.

"Do we actually know where we are going in Sakarra?" Hagar asked.

"I'll call Zein when we get off the bridge," Grace said, fishing her phone out of her purse.

"Zein? That means Shams will definitely be there. Grace, are you sure this is a good idea?" Hagar insisted. She could imagine the long night of drama if the two were to see each other.

Be honest- you were also dreading seeing Zein for the first time after- you know.

"Hagar, fucking chill. It will be fine," Grace said, her thumbs moving fast as she texted furiously. Hagar held back as she looked outside the cab window.

Instead of heading north when exiting the 6th of October bridge, the taxi took a left turn, heading south towards the Sakarra area. Grace called Zein, handing the phone to the cab driver to get exact directions to the drop-off point. Zein, like Shams, was half Egyptian, and spoke Arabic fluently. Hagar could hear the drone of Zein's voice as he guided the cab driver down the canal road.

This side of Giza was less refined than up north where the Giza pyramids were. The canal road was just that- a narrow dirt road that lined either side of a canal dug from the Nile to provide water to the Sakarra area. Bumping along the road, the scenery outside the taxi window changed drastically from that of Cairo on the other side of the river. Short walls built from caked sand and bricks lined plots of land. Most of the agriculture was date farms- one could see the towering trees on all sides of the road, creating a narrow corridor that briefly blocked one's view of the sky. They passed these plots of date farms, some with horse stables attached. Large villas, modern and old, were nestled against lots owned by poorer farmers passed down generations. The taxi driver took a right, weaving into another narrow dirt road lined on one side with train tracks. Hagar didn't know where exactly they were, and wondered how they were planning on leaving Sakkara whenever they were ready to go home. She turned to Grace to ask that every question when they halted at a large villa, the cab driver signaling for them to get out. After briefly haggling over the cab fee again, Hagar asked for the cab driver's number, telling him they would need a ride back across the river if he will service the Sakarra area for a few hours. The cab driver nodded, rolled his window up and left.

Hagar turned to find Grace energetically bopping around Zein and a group of high schoolers. Hagar nodded a hello at Zein, who smiled widely and gave her a side hug with one arm. Whew, okay, maybe he has already forgotten. Apprehension replaced her relief as they walked past an elaborate iron gate to the house. Hagar felt this crowd differed from the usual. There were hardly any Americans present- mostly Egyptian High School students she didn't recognize, and most of the crowd was definitely older. Despite fitting in to the demographic of the party goers better than Grace did, Hagar continued to feel uncomfortable as she followed Grace and Zein to the back of the house. Then the walls opened up to the wide, dark desert. Hagar could see the sand dunes rising immediately in front of them, lit by the glow of the yellow lights from the villa. They parked a row of four wheelers in front of them- Zein motioned for the two girls to jump into the back of one as it revved on. He opened the glove box in the front and pulled out two checkered *kaffiyas*, handing them to the girls..

"Trust me, you'll want them with the sand and the wind," Zein chuckled as he watched Grace don the *kaffiya* with disgust. Hagar giggled at Grace- she had tied the scarf around the bottom half of her face like a cowboy would wear his bandanna, unaware of how to wrap the scarf around her ears and the top of her head to keep her hair down the way the bedouins did it. Hagar was used to wrapping *kaffiyas* around her face from times she had gone riding in the Pyramids desert with her mother, and reached across to adjust Grace's scarf. Once adjusted, Zein revved the four wheelers engine loudly, and they were off into the desert.

Hagar looked up as soon as the villa's lights were out of sight, her feelings of unease immediately replaced with a profound sense of peace. The sky was brilliantly clear that night, a rarity for the desert outside of Giza and the sprawl of the larger Cairo city area. A hazy mist usually hung over the city. The combination of harsh street lights, headlights from cars and trucks jammed on the streets, and bright and festive string lights adorning buildings and balconies along with pollution in the air usually masked the night sky from Cairenes' evenings. The sky was clearer out here in the Sakkara desert, although not as clear as the sky at the farm, Hagar noted.

Zein followed tracks along a desert path that wound between the dunes. In front of them, Hagar saw a handful of small Sakkara step pyramids. The pyramids rarely look majestic during the day- they were short, in various states of crumbling, and the same color as the sand. But this was a rave, complete with a stage with a DJ and a trippy light show that lit up the step pyramid in a way Hagar had never experienced.

"Shit, that is beautiful!" Hagar said once her *kafiyya* was off her face. Zein had parked the ATV in a row next to others, waiting to transport rave goers back to the villa.

"Dork," Grace giggled at Hagar as they dismounted into the deep, cool sand. Hagar shrugged and said nothing in reply. Grace was already distractedly talking to a group of people as Zein fumbled with the keys and lock of the ATV behind Hagar. I guess there is a benefit to even being the ex-girlfriend of Shams, Hagar thought. Grace still knew many, many more people than Hagar did. It was bound to happen after dating someone who felt like the most popular person on the block for two years.

Hagar waited awkwardly, standing close to Zein and the ATV. Not realizing she still had the kafiyya on, Hagar's fingers ran through the pompoms on the fringe of the scarf, trying to untangle them from hours of blowing in the wind. She spaced out on the stars in the sky, looking up but not too far- even with the bright lights coming from the rave's stage, the stars glowed low on the horizon.

Hagar felt a light punch on her shoulder blade as she jumped with surprise. Zein was behind her, grinning, finally done with the ATV. Hagar smiled awkwardly then abruptly looked ahead of her for Grace.

"Hey, cousin," Zein said, grasping Hagar's elbow softly. Hagar hesitated, then looked up at him. He was smiling. I guess I should smile back too. Hagar smiled tersely, uncomfortable with the truth of the nickname.

"It's totally cool, man. I know the news must have been a shock to you. It was definitely to me," he said coolly, looking ahead at Grace still talking animatedly to the group in front of them.

"It's fine," Hagar said, a bit too quickly.

Zein turned to her and put both hands on her shoulders, clutching them. Hagar seemed to shrink into herself, unsure what to do. This was the most conversation the two had had since they had known one another.

"If you need someone to talk to, I'm here," he said.

Hagar shook her head furiously left to right, then slowly nodded immediately after, not wanting to seem unthankful for the gesture. The kaffiyeh blew up into her face and thankfully gave her something to do with her hands. Zein laughed at her awkwardness and pulled her behind him as he grabbed Grace's elbow. He pulled both girls towards the crowd by the stage.

As they approached, Hagar noticed temporary bars set up on either side of the stage- a crowd flocked on both sidesof the stage fighting to grab mixed drinks and beers. Hagar grabbed Grace's hand as they entered the throng. Zein handed each one of them a beer, and retreated to the back of the larger crowd that was packed in front of the stage, swaying to EDM music.

Hagar stood next to Grace and Zein as the two huddled in conversation. The music was too loud to hear what they were saying even though Hagar could see they were yelling. Finally, Zein grabbed Grace's hand and took off into the crowd, Grace giggling. For a moment, Hagar panicked, and rushed to follow them. Then, something stopped her. I don't have to follow her around. She retreated to her spot, and sipped on her beer, taking in the sight of the lights bouncing off of the several thousand year old step pyramid.

She looked down to the crowd, whose faces were temporarily lit in bright white light as the light effects of the show brightened with the quickening beat. She noticed the stumbling, awkward dance moves of a few- others were dancing on their own in a trance, completely in their own worlds without a need for a companion.

It was nothing like the drunk crowds I was used to that Grace had introduced me to with the youth group kids. The drunks were cliquey- they had to be attached to someone all the time, engrossed in conversation. Nobody sat on their own. I was used to being in the back on my own, and never counted myself as being part of what was going on around me. But here, people were acting differently. They were moving slowly, confused, as if in a daze. People were grouped together in couples. But even the couples seemed distant from one another, waving in the light, bathing in the sound. Being alone seemed alright in this crowd- and Hagar kind of liked it.

"It's the drugs," a voice said behind her, right in her ear. She could feel the breath of the speaker float down her exposed chest, and she whirled around. Her heart beat faster when she saw who it was- Shams. His eyes wandered all over her body, scanning her up and down and finally resting on her chest. The kaffiyeh Hagar was still wearing had blown away in the wind, revealing her budding chest and low-cut shirt. He finally made eye contact with her- she remained awkwardly standing, not sure what to say. `He never talked to me, even when he and Grace were together. What do I do??`

"You look good tonight, Hagar. Rare form. What happened, did Grace dress you up?" He smirked as he grabbed the beer from Hagar's hands and took a sip. Her heart raced even faster.

She almost blurted out that the shirt was actually a hand-me-down from Grace, then stopped herself. *No, you idiot.* She looked away from him shyly, taking another sip of her beer.

"I assume you're here with *her*," he pressed, standing next to Hagar, facing the stage.

"Yeah," Hagar finally responded. "Have you seen her yet?"

Shams looked at her sideways, smirking. "Nah, I'm over that bitch. Besides," he paused again, looking Hagar up and down again, making her blush. "You're here."

`I'm here? Since when has that mattered?`

Hagar, take a break. Your crush has noticed you for the first time. Flirt back!

Hagar smiled coyly back at Shams, then her smile froze awkwardly at the thought-

`How the fuck do I flirt?`

She shook her head and looked back at Shams.

"So, do you have any?" she asked. *Hagar, what are you doing?*

"Any what?" Shams asked, a half smile on his face as he moved closer to her. "Drugs?"

Hagar paused, a hot rush going through her body, burning at the nape of her neck where she could feel Shams' breath on her again.

"Yeah," she said nonchalantly.

His smile got wider. "Fuck, maybe you were the cooler one out of the two of you." He reached into his pocket. "Grace would never do this stuff with me."

Hagar's blood ran cold this time as she thought of Grace.

Shams is Grace's ex-boyfriend, what am I doing?

You had a crush on him first, Hagar. They are broken up- there is nothing wrong with you flirting a bit.

But what will Grace say if she finds out?

Grace is lost in the crowd- she doesn't give a shit about what you're doing anyway. You got her out here.

Hagar watched as Shams produced a joint and lit it. Figure it out later? But she never did that. What if her mom woke up? What if her parents found out? It was already late enough- she had to get home in a couple of hours before it was dawn.

Shams inhaled deeply, and looked at her sideways, smiling. The DJ set was using warm lights now, softly pulsing on and off to a slower velvety electronica song. The beat of the song seemed to match her heartbeat as she took the joint from Shams, preparing to inhale.

"It's not like a cigarette," he whispered in her ear, moving closer to her. His chest was touching her right shoulder, his body turned towards her. "Inhale it and keep it in your mouth, then slowly open your throat. Let it roll out slow, like honey."

She looked up into his eyes, hers full of questioning and uncertainty. She smiled nervously then inhaled. After a few years of smoking shisha, it came somewhat naturally to her. She lifted her head, inhaling the smoke slowly, closing her eyes briefly. Like honey.

A few seconds later, she opened her eyes. Shams was facing her directly. She could feel his long, frizzly curls brushing her own curly blonde bangs. Hagar looked into his eyes, offering the joint back. She lifted the joint up higher, as if to place it in between his lips.

I don't know what I am doing.

Panic. Panic. Panic.

As the soft electronica song came to its final chorus, she felt Shams' lips on her fingers as she placed the joint in his mouth. He inhaled, keeping his gaze locked onto hers. She could feel both of his hands creeping onto her hips, pulling Grace's old top up from where it was tucked into her jeans. She tried to control the goosebumps that appeared where she felt his hands touch her waist. It was light at first- just his fingertips. As he finished inhaling, her hands still on his lips, he pulled her arm down with one hand, and using the other, grabbed her neck under the fluff of the kafiyya fringe and pulled her towards him.

As the soft beats faded around them, in the darkness away from the stage, she closed her eyes as she smelled the sweet smell of weed meet her lips. She dropped the joint in the sand, pulled both of her hands up to his hair, grabbing handfuls of the curls she had admired for so long, and continued following his lead, kissing him repeatedly.

When they came up for air, Shams pulled away with slight astonishment on his face. She smiled at him crookedly.

`Did I fuck this up?`

For a second, she thought about Grace and almost broke her gaze with Shams, the urge to frantically search for her in the crowd tugging at her chest. Before she could avert her gaze, Shams grabbed her hand and pulled her closer to the stage, running his hands over her body as they swayed to the next song.

Nope, looks like you did just fine.

Weekend Activities
Cairo

The events at the rave led to a secret romance between Hagar and Shams- secret because, in Hagar's mind, Grace must never find out. Hagar was also wary of other people at youth group, and had demanded Shams keep their relationship a secret. While she did not enjoy secret-keeping, there was some element of thrill for Shams that might have not been present between him and Grace that the secrecy introduced. Hagar went unnoticed as she was absent for breaks in between classes. She and Shams would sneak behind school buildings to make out and giggle in whispers. The very weekend after the rave, Shams invited Hagar out drinking at the grassy knoll, a spot well known as a last resort for high schoolers to go drinking. The first Thursday night, Hagar snuck out of her house late at night, taking a taxi to meet Shams at the spot for the first time. The grassy knoll was unimpressive- a run down garden area that lined the back side of Road 9, close to all of the large villas that were either embassies or housed embassy dignitaries and their families. In this part of town, the streets were narrow, lined with tall trees that seemed to bow in towards one another on either side, creating a green tunnel above the checkered black and white sidewalks. The narrow green corridors echoed of past luxury with majestic old buildings looming behind the line of tall trees, surrounded by decrepit gardens. Hagar never knew why that particular spot along that street had been picked as a hang out spot for high schoolers and select middle schoolers for drinking- there were plenty of other spots, even almost identical gardens that were better taken care of. But never mind that, she thought that first weekend after the rave as she headed to the grassy knoll. `I have a boyfriend now.`

They drank there Thursday night, just the two of them, mostly making out but catching a word or two here and there in between. Then they went there again Friday night. They even met during the week. The first time Shams invited Hagar out during the week, she was hesitant. What would they do? Drink during the week? How would she manage that with her mother and brother at home? But never mind that- under the guise of going to Grace's house or going to the cafe with Hakim, Hagar snuck out to the grassy knoll and began drinking during the week. It became hard for her to remember how many nights a week she was drinking- but when it came to spending time with Shams, it seemed like alcohol was always on hand.

While the secrecy had them enamored for some time, Shams finally decided they needed to socialize. Hagar was concerned, but it was hard to say no when Shams had his arms around her.

"Look, I am having a party at my house this Friday night. My parents will be out on some church trip thing. Some of the guys will come over. Don't worry- Grace doesn't know, she won't be invited."

Hagar paused. She knew that even if Grace wasn't invited, that didn't mean she wouldn't show up. She knew Grace was close to Zein, and Zein would surely be there.

"I don't know…" Hagar said, her voice drifting off as she bit one of her nails in thoughtfulness.

Shams scoffed and reached over, pulling one of her wiry blonde curls behind her ear.

"At this point, so what if Grace finds out? It doesn't seem like she has been missing you around anyways. It's been months since her and I broke up- at some point I'm supposed to move on, right?" he pulled out a cigarette from one of his pockets. He offered Hagar one. She looked at him questioningly- he had never smoked in front of her let alone offered her a cigarette.

So what, you're a smoker now?

Shut up.

Hagar accepted the cigarette from him and leaned in towards him as he offered her his light.

He wasn't wrong about Grace. She hadn't seemed to notice Hagar's absence from weekend activities with her. Hagar went over to Grace's house a few times, but the amount of time they were spending together was noticeably diminished. Grace had not said anything, and invites to any weekend activities she was doing were not extended to Hagar any longer.

"Okay, then," Hagar said after inhaling. She instantly felt dizzy. But it was a good dizzy feeling- it went well with the alcohol. "Fuck it, you're right. If she finds out, she finds out."

Shams smiled at her, and leaned in to bite her ear. How could she say no?

But what if all of the luster of us being together goes away when the secrecy is gone? Then what? Will I be discarded just like Grace was?

Do you have any choice but to find out?

Hagar giggled anxiously as Shams continued to bite her ear, already mentally preparing herself for the upcoming Friday.

***

I remember standing by the door to the balcony, outside staring at the crescent moon hanging from the clouds, its profile skinny against the sky that was lit from all the lights in the city. Growing up I cared more about the crescent moon than I ever did the full moon- the crescent moon had more meaning. It marked the start of the Ramadan fast each year, with each Middle Eastern country anxiously watching when the moon would reach its nadir, the lowest profile marking the start of the long month of fasting.

I was smoking. I needed to get away from the others. Shams was wandering around somewhere, and all I could think of was avoiding Grace when she finally showed up. Because, despite Shams' promises that Grace wasn't invited, I knew she would show up.

Which she did. Her giggling broke my reverie with the moon.

"Where have you been?!" she cooed, looking at me up and down. I was wearing yet another one of her hand-me-downs. "It looks fucking good!" she said, some surprise in her voice.

Then it happened, and it made my heart sink. Shams came out to the balcony, looking for me. He had two mixed drinks in his hand- he handed me one, nodding at Grace. Her face- she was so confused, watching Shams' every move. Her hazel eyes looking at me questioningly, wondering when the hell Shams had paid attention to me, let alone acknowledge my existence at all. I didn't look at her- instead; I remember asking Shams what was in the drink. He smiled at me crookedly. "What, you don't trust me? It's good, try it"- and it was. I kept sipping at it for the next few seconds, pretending like I wasn't there at all. Instead of disappearing back into his house, though, Shams put his arms around me. I could feel Grace's eyes- they got wider, the widest I had ever seen them. It was a warm night, and in a matter of seconds it felt like the heat emanating from the cement sidewalk below began melting her eyeliner and eyeshadow- their slickness oozed into the crow's feet that accented her eyes.

People started filing out to the balcony to join Shams, never giving Grace a chance to react. As people crowded between Shams and I and her, she eventually faded to the back. I lost track of her, but I knew, I could feel that she was mad.

I sipped on my drink a little faster.

The next thing I remember was Shams leading me down a hallway. We ended up in a bedroom- maybe it was his? It wasn't clear- everything in the apartment looked the same, none of the furniture or pictures anywhere seemed to speak to one member of his family or the other. This room had a perfect view of the Nile, unlike the balcony in the back that had been looking East over the rest of the city. Only then did I realize just how high the apartment was. The dark slithering Nile was below us, the lights twinkling below. I remember looking out and smiling, thinking he had brought me here for the view.

But then his hands wandered... he turned me around, facing him. He took my jacket off... then his hands were under my shirt.

This was the farthest we had ever gone.

My heart beat a little faster.

He took my shirt - Grace's old shirt- off and suddenly I felt cold, open, naked. I reached for my drink to distract myself from what was happening. My head felt dizzy and tired. I looked at the bed in the room- it looked so inviting, and the rest was tempting. He saw me looking at the bed, and grinned, pulling me to it, then pulling me down...

And that was the last thing she felt, consciously anyway. Going down, down into Shams' arms. We both fell together, then darkness- complete blackness. I seemed to float above her- them- as I often do when she feels so far away from me. Her body was limp, but his was not. It stood, erect, tight, ready- accepting of her giving up, giving in- or so it seemed.

Then we went to sleep.

The Nadir
Cairo

She woke up and there were leaves in her hair.

Her head- her eyes- were killing her. She looked about, then looked down- she was still in the same clothes from last night. Her hands smeared black- it took her a moment to realize it was her own makeup. She was in her room, in bed, under the covers. She closed her eyes.

What happened? How did I get here?

She moved to get up from the bed and looked down- her jeans were ripped.

What the fuck happened last night?

Then...

Shit. Where is mom?

Hagar got out of bed. Her door was closed and locked. She frowned at the lock, twisted the key and yanked the door open. She peeked out into the hallway, looking left and right to see if anyone was up. Hearing nothing, she scooted to the bathroom.

I have to shower before anyone sees me.

She showered and changed, apprehension still hanging over her. Her head was feeling horrible still, her stomach felt like it was floating and out of sync from the rest of her body. She realized her throat, which felt like something had been scratching it for days. It was dry, and it hurt. There was a dull soreness in between her legs, burning like a UTI.

Dehydration? She rubbed her neck- I need a drink of water- and stepped out of the bathroom into the hallway, heading to the kitchen. The house was eerily quiet.

As she tip-toed to the kitchen, the sight of her mother caught her immediately. She was sitting at the dining room table with a cup of coffee in her hand, consternation on her face. She was facing the hallway, still in her PJ's, unusual for her mother even for a Friday morning. Hagar paused before going into the kitchen. Her mother's gaze shifted up at Hagar. The deep gray of the mother's eyes weighed heavy.

They were heavy with disappointment.

Fuck. She knew.

"Sit down," Hagar's mother said firmly, gesturing towards the chair opposite her.

Hagar sat down without question and noticed a glass of water was already waiting for her.

***

"I found you at the hospital. Wherever you had gone- whatever you had been drinking- it was bad. Bad alcohol. You weren't the only one there- some girl from the French high school- she went blind. They pumped your stomach. That's when I got the call from the hospital. And it doesn't stop there. You had sex- sex with someone. One girl at the hospital said she found you without your clothes on, lying in a bed. She had helped you put your clothes back on when she realized you were past any point of getting yourself home alone reliably. She found you alone- nobody else was there. "

The mother was ashamed, having to explain to us what happened to us, and we didn't even remember. She probably never thought she would have a problem with her daughter like this.

The mother shook her head. There was nothing else to tell. Hagar was lucky to be alive.

And Hagar was no longer a virgin.

"Oh, and also," the mother said as Hagar got up, glass of water still clutched in her hands. "Your father knows. I would expect a visit from him sometime today." Her voice was resigned. Hagar and her mother locked eyes- they knew what this meant.

"Everything? He knows everything?" Hagar asked, her voice squeaking with fear.

"Everything," the mother said, her voice monotone.

Hagar's heart dropped.

No, please no.

***

There was not even a knock at her door. Hours later, her room door came crashing open. It was just about dinner time- about the time the father came home, if he was coming home at all. And he was here.

Hagar cringed as she spilled hot tea on her lap, and all over the novel she was reading. She was about to turn around in annoyance, but the deep throbbing in the back of her head kept her spinning.

"YOU- OUTSIDE," the father boomed, holding the door open at first, then bending down and grabbing Hagar by the arm, spilling more tea.

"برة!"

"OUT!"

Hagar almost said something about him grabbing her with hot tea in her hand, but realized there was no point. This fight would not be like the others.

Hagar walked out of her room, and the father shoved her down the hallway. She came to the dining room to find her mother sitting there already, tears streaming down her face.

This will not be good.

The father shoved Hagar down into a chair, pushing it up so

close to the table with a shove that it hurt her ribs. Hagar winced, but kept her mouth shut.

"I know… everything," the father whispered angrily in her ear. "Everything- I mean EVERYTHING your mother and you have been hiding from me for years!"

Hagar cringed.

The father pulled out a chair at the table and sat down, his demeanor suddenly changed to a calm sea after the storm. Hagar looked at him, wondering what was next. Was that it? Was it over?

They sat in silence for a few minutes, and finally the mother piped up.

"For heaven's sake get this over with," she mumbled, leaning forward on the table. "This is ridiculous, this act you put us through."

"Ridiculous?!" the father boomed, his voice loud again, his demeanor turned from angry to aggressive. Hagar cowered back slightly, expecting him to hit her. "Ridiculous? You know what is ridiculous? Our daughter! And what she has become!" he was spitting, his words forced, as if searching for harsher alternatives to use. "I TOLD you, mom, I TOLD you she would turn into a mess! But I listened to you, anyway! Why? Because you're the mother, you told me," mimicking the mother's voice.

"Oh, like hell. The kids at her old school get into the same shit. Except it's mostly drugs and not alcohol. Don't pretend like this is something that comes to you as a total surprise. Kids get in trouble, dad, where have you been?" the mother's voice rose with irritation. Tears were still streaming down her face, the words came out as angry sobs. Hagar had never seen her like this- this perplexed.

"Like *eh*? What is that word you used? You do not speak to me like this! Women do not raise their voices like this! It is *eib*! It is forbidden for a wife to raise her voice to her husband!"

When dad was angry, he always made fun of

mom's English idioms- mostly because he didn't understand them. I know she did it on purpose- to aggravate him, crawl under his skin. Each time she did, it scratched away at the old wound that kept reopening with regret; regret that he married a Christian American woman, and that he did not fully understand her nor could he control her.

He couldn't control her... Maybe like he controlled his other wife. Maybe she was easier to control.

Yes. The way Egyptian men always control their wives.

I would always have something to say when the fights started. I would fight just as hard as my father. Some fights, mother never said a word. But there was something in the air that was different that night, an extra charge of electricity that made the whites of my father's eyes glow bright.

The father redirected his attention to Hagar.

"YOU. It's YOU we are fighting about. You stupid, non-believing slut! You know alcohol is haram! You know that these- these stupid kids you were with- they are trouble!"

His eyes darted from left to right, unable to hold Hagar's gaze. Hagar was quiet, calm- tired. She was exhausted. She was no longer tuned in to the conversation- I followed her as we wandered elsewhere. Not anywhere in particular, just winding roads where she yearned to end up asleep in her room...

"These kids- these kids all go to church together!" the father said. "I went all the way back to the *bawwab* at the boy's house- what is his name- Shams- the *bawwab* told me everything! That the boy's father is a pastor at the church! That you had been in and out of that building with him for *months*!"

The father pounded the table, irritated at the lack of response from Hagar and the mother. Both jumped briefly, and- satisfied with the desired effect, the father stood up from his seat.

"But the worst part- the WORST PART- is what I found out at the church. That's right. I spent all night investigating- driving like a crazy madman. I went to the church and the policeman who was there- he is undercover police- said he had seen you at multiple gatherings these- these heathens have- what do they call them? *Groups*! At people's houses!"

"See Hagar- what you and these stupid people don't know is that the secret police- they are everywhere. They know everything. And when I told this policeman that I was your father- a devout, Muslim man with our own mosque even!- he was ready to come arrest you. Arrest you!"

He inhaled deeply.

"What you have done is not just bad like your stupid mother says- it is multiple, multiple crimes! These are crimes! A Muslim girl spending time with Christians in their heathen worship, and drinking alcohol!"

"I am not Muslim," Hagar said, breaking the silence her and the mother had espoused since the argument had started. "I am not Muslim. These are not crimes."

The mother put her head in between her hands. The nightmare would never end.

"WHAT?" the father yelled. "What do you think you are saying? That you are not Muslim! You don't have a *choice*! You are my daughter, a direct descendent from the prophet himself!" the father spat, his hand up with a single finger pointed to the sky, as if he was poking the underbelly of the prophet himself. "You don't have a choice, Hagar. You cannot choose for yourself- you are not a heathen like your mother, here," he gestured at the mother suddenly, knocking her forearm. "You are not like this horrible woman here!" he repeated.

Hagar was about to stand, to defend her mother- but there was no need. The mother shot up from her seat instead; her face donning the blank look of total and complete anger that Hagar had only seen a few times.

"That. Is. Enough," she said. "This is not about me- this is about your- *our* daughter. I already know you hate me- you don't need to reiterate this! Yell at her, do what you need to do, and leave this house! We have had enough as it is in the past twenty-four hours, we don't need more of *this!*"

He shot up from his chair, reached across the table, grabbed mom's arm, and slapped her face. I faintly recall him pulling her hair, as if they were children in the playground in disagreement. Mother's face- it was a moment in time frozen in my memory. The mother's lips pressed together, a ring of white around her mouth. Her eyes squeezed shut, and her forehead was red. Her face- it was bracing for pain and full of pain at the same time. I felt a surge of rage and dashed in between them. Maybe I thought father wouldn't touch me, but all I cared about was to get her away from him. I used all the strength I had- which wasn't much, my head still throbbing- and shoved him away. Somehow it worked- he crashed into the wicker sofa behind him, almost losing his balance and falling to the floor.

Hagar and her mother stood, grasping each other's arms.

The father locked eyes with him as he straightened up standing, pulling his collared plaid shirt over his fat belly.

"That's it," he said, low and shaky with anger. "You are no longer my daughter! I will have the papers drawn up today by my lawyer! I am done with you!" he wiped his mouth from all the spit that was generated with each word forced out of his mouth. "This will not absolve me in the eyes of Allah your actions will lead me straight to hell- but I have done the most I have to show Allah that I have separated myself from your evil, evil ways that you have decided will be your life!"

"Good," Hagar spat, breathless. "Good. Now go away and

leave us *alone!*"

"US," the father laughed suddenly. "US? You, Hagar, are on your own. Your mother is also on her own. Thank Allah for Bakry," he said.

The father turned on his heels, facing the hallway behind him. He was about to walk down the hallway, probably to go check the bedrooms for Bakry. But he didn't need to- Bakry was standing at the end of the hallway, eyes large, countenance scared. He looked like a wet rat left exposed in the rain with nowhere to hide.

"Come on!" the father yelled, grabbing Bakry by the arm. "You are coming with me, son." Bakry initially seemed willing to go, then as the pair made it closer to the front door, the father dragging the son behind him, Bakry began to cry.

The father finally released the boy, shoving him to the ground. Bakry crumpled, the right side of his body unable to balance him against the father's strength. The mother rushed to the crumpled heap at the father's feet, pulling him away as she shied away from the father's grasp.

"I hope Allah sends all of you straight to hell," the father spat, turning one last time towards the door, opening it, then slamming it shut. Hagar rushed to her mother and Bakry.

"Get out of my sight," the mother hissed. Hagar cowered and drifted back towards her room.

***

Hagar spent the rest of the weekend in her room with the door closed, only leaving to fetch food or water from the kitchen or go to the bathroom. Shame followed her everywhere. While Bakry didn't know the details of what had happened- but he knew Hagar was in trouble and didn't stop his sideways smiles and smirks at her whenever they crossed paths in the house. The mother showed a clear deference towards the boy, tending to his every need, even making him dinner. Hagar scowled in response and disappeared as quickly as she could back to the safety of her room.

Her thoughts swirled in vicious circles that weekend, wondering what had happened the night she blacked out. She felt far away from her family- but this was not unusual. Instead, she dwelled on the events that had happened in her chosen circle of friends- the people she would have to face at school. She spent hours lying in bed, trying to piece together events from the evening. But as hard as she tried, the last and only thing she could remember was laying down in a bed with Shams next to her.

I was obsessed with the idea of the door being open. Was it open? Had we closed it? Who was this girl who found her? How many people had seen her, lying there naked and passed out? Had Shams been there with her?

I don't remember. I was out, just like you were. What were you thinking, Hagar? Drinking that much? And drinking liquor at that! You had always stuck with beer- and it should have stayed that way.

I was fucking nervous, okay? I was nervous because I knew -

-You knew Grace would be there. So what, Hagar? You had hidden behind Shams long enough- Grace would have found out, eventually.

I know. I just didn't want to lose her. And now here I am - without friends and potentially half of the high school having seen me naked in bed at a party.

The following Sunday, Hagar drew in a big breath as she entered the front gate. Nobody was paying attention to her- that is until she reached the high school section.

How many people know?

Probably everyone. I mean, everyone was at Shams' party.

Hagar hid behind the bagel stand, knowing that half of the people who were at the party were lined up to grab their morning bagel and smoothie.

You're going to have to face them at some point.

`Not if I time it right.`

Once the bell rang, class would start in ten minutes. Hagar waited. A few minutes past eight, she scrambled to her locker, grabbed her binder, and headed to class. As she rushed through the door for class, it felt like everyone was looking her up and down.

`How many of them had seen me- all of me?`

She stole a glance at Grace's desk. She was there, but making no eye contact to acknowledge Hagar's late entry into class. Hagar's usual desk next to Grace was still left open, but Hagar decided against sitting there, wandering meekly to the back of the classroom and grabbing a seat in the last row.

"Well Hagar, this is mighty unusual," the English teacher boomed, his British accent cheery against her dark mood. He was used to Hagar, one of his most eager students, being in the front row. The class was an advanced placement English course, and he knew how much she loved literature. But today, not a single British classic would have brought her to the front of the room to take her place next to Grace. Dr. Bryant, sensing the unease in Hagar's movements as she settled in, decided against throwing his dry, British humor her way. Today things felt different.

Hagar stared at the back of Grace's head for the entire class, wondering if she would ever speak to her ever again.

***

While Hagar was grounded from all social activities for the foreseeable future, her mother allowed her to continue attending youth group. At first Hagar decided not to go- the weight would be too heavy, the looks too many. Besides, the only friends she had at youth group were Grace and Shams- both of which Hagar was sure wouldn't speak to her. Shams had never returned her calls or texts- he clearly got what he wanted from me at the party. Then she remembered Boure's cheerful spirit- how she had always told Hagar she could reach out anytime, even when things were bad with Hagar's father. As Monday and Tuesday passed, Hagar figured the least she could do was go to youth group Wednesday night with the hope that Boure would be available to speak in private.

And so Hagar trudged to youth group that night- climbed the stairs, greeted by Boure with her usual enthusiasm. This time, Hagar asked if she could speak with Boure privately.

"Of course, little lady! Let's go over here away from the stage- Travis is being obnoxious with his new guitar!"

Hagar followed her to a corner of the rooftop. She was aware of many stares- most of them incredulous at the idea that Hagar would show up to youth group at all.

Hagar faced Boure, whose countenance had changed slightly.

"Boure... I'm sure you know what happened," Hagar stuttered.

"I know," Boure responded with a solemn look on her face. "Hagar, what would make you go to a party like that? I mean, I know it was at Shams' house and Shams hosted it- just because it is Shams and his father is the pastor here does NOT mean you should have been there!"

Hagar paused. Wait- does she think only Shams and I were there from the youth group community?

"I-" Hagar stammered. Should she out the rest? *What would be the point, though? They are all judging you enough as it is. That would be a sure way to make sure you never have friends again.*

Boure continued. "Girl I know you have *a lot* going on- you always have. Between what you have told me and what Grace has told me- I *so feel* for you in your position right now. But alcohol and partying and sex will solve none of those things- you know this!"

Literally every other person who is here was there too.

"Girl, I am always here to help you and I am praying for you so hard right now. Maybe this was His way of giving you a wake up call to work on your own life in more positive ways. Everyone has their burdens- it's what you do that matters!" Boure smiled widely, placing a hand on Hagar's shoulder. "Now, before we start the group, let's say a brief prayer, just the two of us. "

Hagar, still speechless, nodded slowly as if responding on autopilot. Boure lifted her arms and rubbed Hagar's shoulders vigorously as if to warm the girl up. The rubbing went still as Boure bowed her head in prayer. Normally, Hagar would have bowed her head. But this time- this time, she felt frozen in place.

"Dear Lord, I want to pray for this precious gem in front of me who has had such a series of unfortunate events. Jesus, I pray for Hagar as she continues her journey to and with you; as she battles evil forces at home from non-believers, as she tries to obey and love her mother, and as she fights alcohol as a potential way to deal with these challenges. Jesus, I hope you show her the way to your light- how alcohol and drugs and sex are not the answer, but temporary sinful satisfactions that do not bring any love or joy to the world. I hope you keep your eyes and protective arms around her during this time, and I hope you shepherd her towards us, the students and youth pastors here who can help her along her journey and provide the love, support and guidance that she needs as she navigates these challenging events. Amen."

Hagar remained silent. She had fixed her stare on the stage the whole time, only half listening to Boure's prayer. Boure looked up at her and forced her into an energetic hug, patted the side of her cheek with a sympathetic look on her face, then walked back to the door by the stairway to greet others. Hagar's blood ran cold when she saw Grace come through the door-Grace's demeanor cheerful upon seeing Boure. Her expression went flat when she made eye contact with Hagar, who was approaching.

`I have to tell her I am sorry.`

"Grace…" Hagar tapped on Grace's shoulder gently as Grace was turning towards the stage. Grace whirled around, already angry at hearing Hagar's voice.

"What do you want?"

"Just to talk. To tell you I am sorry. About Shams. About everything really."

Grace rolled her eyes. "Yeah? Everything? You have no idea how much you have fucked things up," Grace turned to face Hagar. "Not only did you fuck my ex-boyfriend, but you lost your virginity before marriage AND now everyone's parents are being super strict because YOU were an idiot, drank too much and got caught."

"Listen, I am sorry, ok? I was drinking liquor that night because I was nervous about the whole Shams thing, and I didn't want to piss you off."

"Oh, so now it's *my* fault that you were drinking? You know what Hagar," Grace inhaled deeply. "You need to take ownership of your own fucking problems. Yeah, life for you is fucked up- but it has made you blame all of your problems on literally everyone else except for yourself. Grow up. This whole thing was your fault because you couldn't keep your pants on, you fuck other people's ex-boyfriends and are now basically an alcoholic." Grace shook her head. "I want nothing to do with you. I am sure most people here don't. So - *fuck off.*"

Hagar stood in place, aghast as Grace turned on her heels and walked towards the stage. Hagar saw her walk up to Shams and give him a hug- and he hugged her back. Hurt and confusion engulfed Hagar's senses- she couldn't believe her eyes, and her heart seemed to have stopped in place.

Get out of here.

She turned to the door that led down the stairway and took the stairs two at a time, running home as fast as she could.

Sisyphus
Cairo

Hagar slung her Jansport backpack over her shoulder. The bell rang- biology class was over. Hagar looked up from packing her bookbag, hoping to catch Hakim's glance. Since moving to the American school, Hakim had found his own circle of friends. His move didn't happen until high school, when his parents were sufficiently satisfied that Hakim had received the foundation in religion and Arabic studies. While he invited her to spend time with them, Hagar did not quite feel like she fit in.

Hakim was deep in conversation, so Hagar left the classroom. She walked outside to the locker area to drop off her heavy biology binder. After slamming the locker door shut, she turned towards the gate to walk home when Hakim caught up with her.

"How are you holding up?"

He knew about the party and Shams, and that Hagar and Grace had a falling out. I mean, everyone knew all the details.

Hagar shook her head. "I am tired," she said with a crooked smile.

"Here, I'll walk you home. Let's grab some coffee on our way," Hakim said, motioning towards the bagel stand. Hagar nodded gratefully.

She and Hakim walked in silence. After grabbing a coffee each from the bagel stand, they walked towards Hagar's house.

Both admired the spring blooms that had sprung from the trees that surrounded the outer wall of the school. Hagar especially loved the bougainvillaea that lined the sidewalks. Their little purple, orange and white crepe flowers peeked out from under the heavily thorned green branches, elegantly trimmed. At the center of each bloom would be a miniature cream-white flower stemming from the crepe petals around it as if to keep the larger flower company.

"I can't believe people are already looking at colleges," Hakim piped up, attempting to fill the silence. "It's like- we still have two years, but everything goes so fast between now and then."

"I can't wait," Hagar said.

"Have you decided about which schools you will apply to?" Hakim asked.

Hagar shook her head. "I'm still so undecided on what I want to study. I did okay in my photography show, a big part of me wants to go into some type of design… I have been looking at London School of Design … but then, I think of astrophysics and astronomy- I would love to study the stars- but mom said I won't make any money that way," Hagar's hands went up in despair. "I just don't know."

"So- you're looking at England- like me!"

Hakim smiled.

"Well, yeah… for now. Except for the money thing."

Hagar looked at Hakim with unease.

"There is no way we can afford any of the schools that I am looking at… and the likelihood of me getting a scholarship as the ton of Arabs trying to get into uni in Europe… I don't know."

Hakim waved his hand, batting away the unease of the subject of scholarships that had floated between them. As they approached Hagar's house, he faced her with a twinkle in his eye.

"If you end up leaving Egypt, just don't forget…" he said, a smirk crawling across his face slowly.

Hagar rolled her eyes.

"That I am a Khalifa," they said simultaneously, giggling together.

"It always sounds better when you say it instead of dad," Hagar said.

She winced at the mention of her father. He is everywhere.

"How *is* your dad?" Hakim asked tentatively.

"Well… he disowned me in so many words."

Hakim scoffed and waved his hand.

"There is no way he follows through with that threat," he said confidently.

Hagar shrugged her shoulders as she leaned over and hugged Hakim, turning to go upstairs.

"Thank you, Hakim," she called out as he turned to leave too. "Thank you for always being there."

He smiled and nodded. "Of course, always."

She started up the stairs. She opened the door, expecting the mother and Bakry to be back from school. The house was quiet. Hagar went straight to her room, dropping her heavy book bag on her bed. She noticed a piece of paper folded on her pillow, with her name on one side in her mother's handwriting. She set her cup of coffee down on the nightstand by her bed, gingerly unfolding the note, unsure what to expect.

"Gone to the farm with Bakry for the weekend. Do not go out, do not get in trouble. Signed you up for counseling with one of the high school counselors- you start next Monday.

Mom."

A deep pang of hurt hit Hagar in her chest while reading the first sentence. She took Bakry to the farm instead of her? What happened to them riding horses together?

Well, looks like you have been replaced.

No. That can't be right. Mom probably figured

I had too much homework to do and didn't want to bother asking if I wanted to go for the entire weekend... there is no way I could be gone for that amount of time away from my laptop and Wi-Fi and schoolwork.

Sure... you keep telling yourself that. Especially as you head to counseling next week.

Hagar cringed with anger at the second sentence. Counseling? Did her mother think she was so messed up that she needed counseling? For what? It's not like she was an alcoholic, or was using drugs. She just messed up- once. Hagar tossed the note to the side, shaking her head.

Instead of spending the evening studying the way she needed to, she stared at the note, laying down on her bed, and forced herself to sleep early.

Saul
Cairo

Hagar glared at the counselor sitting in front of her.

"So, what made you drink alone this past weekend? Let's dig into that further. How does it make you feel? After everything that has happened?"

The counselor's eyes squinted slightly as if to encourage the deep critical thought she was hoping her patient was experiencing.

Hagar rolled her eyes, regretting telling the counselor about the drinking. She knew everything she said in their sessions would be confidential, but it gave the counselor the perfect topic to target for the rest of their session.

"I mean, that's what people do when they are going through shit, right? They drink a bit to think. Ernest Hemingway did it. Actually, almost every single famous artist did it. So why is it such a big deal?"

"Well, Hagar, it's mostly because you are in High School and they were not," the counselor said matter of fact.

"Actually, that's not entirely true…"

Hagar was cut off by the counselor.

"Hagar, this is not the point of our discussion," the counselor looked away, exasperated. "Let's move onto a different topic- you said you have been feeling like you are being treated unfairly by people at your youth group. Tell me more about this."

Hagar felt a pang at the pivot. The woman sure knew how to tick her off the most. Hagar's irritability increased. She hated these sessions. Hagar had truly only drank one other time outside of that- the time she just mentioned, alone at night at the grassy knoll. Nobody was there except for Hagar and her bottles of Heineken. It gave her space and time to think.

She looked up at the counselor. Hagar was sitting leaning forward, her hands clasped together in front of her. A position of defeat, she thought. She straightened up to answer the question.

"Fuck the church," Hagar finally said. "Let's talk about something else."

"Well, no wait there, Hagar. This is important," the counselor said. She was African American, her skin a deep chocolate brown. Her almond eyes perfectly lined with eyeliner. Her hair was chopped close to her head, echoes of small tightly wound curls all over. Her lips were a deep magenta- naturally that way, but one could detect the light lip gloss of the same shade. The counselor's perfectly manicured hands gestured towards her notes.

"It sounded like the connections you had at church have been extremely important in helping you through your situation at home. What happened?"

Hagar sneered at the thought of Boure and Grace. It had been weeks since Hagar had sent Boure loads of texts asking for her help. No response. After the small pep talk she had received, both Boure and Grace had gone radio silent. Hagar knew Shams was still going to youth group- of course he would. Rumors were even flying about that he and Grace were back together- that he was sobering up and becoming a better person.

She finally broke the silence.

"They're gone. All gone. They supported me until I was the one to get caught. Out of all the church kids who were at that damn party drinking- it was me who had to take the fall for it."

Hagar made eye contact with the counselor.

"So, if you must know what happened there, what happened was I got kicked out of the church family. No longer welcomed. Totally okay with it. Now that's settled, can we move on?"

The counselor leaned back, taking notes.

"Would you say this has affected your faith?"

Hagar furrowed her eyebrows.

"What are you, some kind of religious counselor?" Hagar asked rudely. "I made it very clear I took you on as my counselor because I didn't want to drag God and all of his nonsense into this. Why are we talking about it then?"

The counselor leaned back and raised her eyebrows, placing her clipboard on the desk next to her. She moved the cursor to the Mac desktop screen, waking it up to check the time. `Oh cool, even this bitch doesn't have time for me.`

"Hagar, I want to try an exercise with you before our session is up. It should help you like this when you feel super irritated. Would you mind trying it?"

Hagar nodded, feeling a tinge of guilt. She didn't mean to be irritable with the counselor. She knew the counselor had no choice but to take Hagar on- in the current state of low self esteem, Hagar couldn't blame her for watching the time.

Straighten up. Listen and cooperate for the last few minutes. You heard her.

"Yeah, sure," Hagar said, looking at the counselor.

"Okay, please get into a comfortable position," the counselor said. "Don't worry, we aren't meditating. We're doing a different exercise- one I want you to try whenever you feel backed into a corner," the counselor said.

"Ok," Hagar agreed, leaned back into the chair and closed her eyes.

"Ok. Now I want you to imagine a scene from your childhood. Something where you felt safe. A place you might have liked when you were young that made you happy."

`Cornfields at the farm. The corn stalks were high above my head. It was the field next to our house- it went for acres and acres.`

"Ok, now I want you to zoom out- instead of being you, I want you to look at the younger you. And I want you to watch her for a second. Watch what she might be doing. Watch her knowing that everything she is doing was something you would do, but you're not her."

She is me, she is young. She is wearing Oshkosh overalls- a light acid wash. Underneath she is wearing a bright marigold yellow shirt. The brightness of the shirt contrasts against her dark caramel colored skin. Her hair is golden and frizzy- like frayed electric wires. Curly-q's pulled away from her face in a red bandana, folded in half and tied at the nape. The early morning sun. The rays are visible against the clear blue sky that echoes of the darkness of night, recently passed.

"Now, watch her. What is she doing?"

The girl is walking through the corn- the steaks cower over her, bending inwards over her head as if embracing her slight frame with their pointy leaves. She is walking slowly, you can feel her smile even though her face is not apparent. You are following her into the cornfield, so all you can see is the back of her head covered by the red bandanna and the Oshkosh logo on the back of her overalls.

"Now I want you to use your five senses. What is she smelling? What is she touching? What is she hearing?"

You can smell the fresh morning air that is a mixture of dewy water droplets and wet sand. There are undertones of manure used to fertilize the field. You can touch the leaves of the cornstalks. They are rough- little hairs sticking out to protect their soft greenish-yellow surface. They tickle her face as she continues to walk behind herself slowly.

"Now, take a moment to talk to this other version of you. Tell her things you want to tell her now that you want her to know. I want these to be statements of affirmation- statements that she doesn't know yet that will make her feel optimistic about the rest of her life. Speak to her."

```
I can't.
```
Ok, I can.

You are going to be stronger for what you go through now.

You are going to be special for what you are going through now.

Everything you will experience moving forward will make you a better, more unique you.

Everything you will experience will be part of your story, no one else's.

All the adversity is there just to prepare you for something more. Something better. I don't know what that is yet, but it is there.

I want to tell you things get better, but I am not sure I can.

```
The younger version of me turned around, smiling.
A gap-toothed smile, both front teeth are gone. A
fat caramel hand reaches up to me, beckoning with a
hand and small, small nails. I take it in mine- I
can feel the act of doing this but cannot see it.
```

Hagar opened her eyes suddenly, tears streaming down her face. Before she let a sob out, she hastily got up from the chair, picked up her Jansport backpack, and hurried out of the counselor's room.

Khan El Khalili
Old Islamic Cairo

A gentle late morning breeze blew through the alleyway. Hagar smiled across the small wooden table as Hakim reached for his glass of sahlab. They both nodded as the man dumped the ashy gray coals on their water pipes into his ladle and retrieved fresh, orange coals pulsing with energy. Hagar stared fixated at the orange glow at the top of her shisha pipe, knowing they would turn ashy as soon as she started inhaling. The server used the small metal tongs deftly, with little regard to whether or not he burned his hands in scooping out fresh coals.

Hagar loved the tradition where shisha servers always waited for a nod of approval before leaving the table, ensuring the new coals had not changed the taste of the pipe. That amount of consideration given to the shisha customer was a deeply appreciated and honored tradition that always left Hagar pleasantly surprised.

Hagar inhaled her shisha pipe after they exchanged her coals and nodded at the server. She picked up her cup of tea and sipped deeply, feeling the warm sweet brown liquid flow into her mouth.

Hagar leaned back in her chair in satisfaction. She was happy at her rekindled her friendship with Hakim that came after the incident. She felt her time was better spent in experiences that made her a better person for them. They would jump into a cab and go anywhere once the weekend came around- they would drive to the outermost fringe of the city's expanse to find the best shisha café or to see a whirling dervish show. Something wholesome- and actually memorable, unlike many of the drinking escapades that were what was left of Hagar's memories of her relationship with Shams.

Their favorite place to wander was Khan El Khalili. A marketplace thousands of years old, it mostly sold trinkets to tourists, but other things always caught Hagar's eyes: colorful rolls of cotton fabric, glass shishas that gleam and change tint in the hot summer sun, alabaster statuettes of all sizes molded and carved into all the Pharaonic gods and goddesses. Tea and coffee shops lining narrow streets and alleyways. El Feshawy, the famous tea shop once frequented by Naguib Mahfouz himself, was the first location of choice to kick off an evening at the Khan.

El Feshawy nested in a narrow walkway. Geometric walls of wooden mashrabiya lined the bottom floor of the cafe, appearing to precariously bolster the weight of the rest of the old building. Only instinct led even the most frequent of cafe goers to El Feshawy. She could never quite articulate directions to another person. She preferred to follow Hakim on such excursions- beginning from the parking garage to the edge of the Khan. The parking garage, a more recent addition to the marketplace as the government's attempt to ease parking woes along narrow streets, on the other side of a four lane road which had to be crossed in order to get to the market. On that road, she felt as if she were standing on the edge of two eras- behind her the tall rectangular silhouettes of skyscrapers, and in front her were old sandstone walls, where muezzins. She always followed Hakim on these excursions- he knew the Khan better than she did. He would duck and weave in between throngs of market-goers. There were always people on the streets, no matter what time of the day. In and out, his hands grasping the strap of her purse, they would pass under ouds and Ramadan lamps hanging from tents of color blocked geometry. The dizzying array of the tent's colors would blend into wooden carton racks full of fresh fruit, the juicing machines whirring a low hum underlining the noise of busy streets. Shin level display cases would be sprawled out on the sidewalks displaying small camels stuffed with sand decorated with gaudy beads, haphazardly protruding into the walkway. She always wondered how shopkeepers made sure nothing was stolen from their sprawling storefront displays, with thousands of busy feet shuffling past their shops. Maybe it was the assurance that the only people who would ever buy such wares were honest tourists, who naively never haggled down prices.

They would duck behind a *galabeyya* shop, and for a moment her senses drowned in the colorful waves of thin cotton and silk blends. Bright magentas, green the color of alfalfa fields in the summer, blue like the color of the Nile of Upper Egypt, deep yellow to match the Egyptian sun, and burnt orange would be the line of the horizon where the sand and sun would meet. Then all light would dim, just a bit, and they would be in front of El Feshawy, taking minced steps to weave in and out of the wooden chairs and tables that lined both sides of the alleyway.

While waiting for a waiter to attend to them, they would sit inside to admire the mirrors that lined the interior of the coffee shop. Every corner was reflective space, taking all the bustle inside the coffee shop and amplifying it into millions of minor scenes.

They bought their backgammon sets at the Khan as well, in the corner of some street at a wood carving shop. She always loved the smell of the store: deep and musty mixed with the heavy humidity of summer.

On one visit to the Khan, they tried to find the highest point in the market. The obvious answer was to climb the minarets. They found one mosque that seemed to be older than the rest. At first the gatekeeper would not let them in; it was after touring hours; he claimed. Hakim began haggling with him in quiet whispers, telling him they weren't tourists, but Egyptian students trying to explore their heritage. This thought must have appealed to the bit of romance hidden in the corner of the man's heart- he disappeared into what looked like a guard shack briefly, then beckoned to them, guiding them to a dark, narrow passage.

The climb to the top was dark and long. Typically reserved for only the *muezzin,* the ascent occurred five times a day for the call to prayer. While Hakim might view the climb as a moment of spiritual tribute, Hagar viewed the climb as an opportunity to lift her head over the flurry of activity below her, find a clear view of the sky, and take a deep breath. Once they had reached the top, she exhaled, imagining her breath could clear the city from the cloak of haze that turned most sharp edges into blurry, questionable lines. Up high was one of the few times Hagar considered the sprawling beauty of the city- her city- contemplating the pride she had in her own heritage for a second, before all the optimism came tumbling down.

Because of course, she couldn't think about her Egyptian heritage without thinking of her father. And now, she couldn't think of her father without thinking about how he had disowned her, how he was ashamed of who she was and who she had become. Tears came to her eyes, but she held them back, in that reservoir where pressure and water can build up behind the eyes, but still hold back tears from flooding the water gates. Her eyes only appeared moist, which Hakim probably figured was from the smoke and haze that engulfed them at the top of the muezzin tower. Maybe even a bit of sentimentality from Hagar at the view- but he doubted that. She wasn't one for sentimentality at these things.

Hagar finally let a light smile come to her lips as they drove back from Old Cairo to their homes in a cab, Hakim sitting in front (because the men always did) and Hagar sitting in the back.

She smirked at the hole at the bottom of the taxi floor in between her feet- `I can relate to that hole in more ways than one;` she thought. Then she looked up at the moon, full and high in the sky. It was almost midnight.

Hagar had received no calls or texts from her mother- she knew Hagar was out with Hakim, comforted because Hakim was safe company for her daughter (and always had been) compared to other alternatives. Hagar waved at Hakim, and walked up the stairs slowly. The lights weren't on in the apartment- the mother and Bakry must be asleep. But as Hagar unlocked the door to the apartment and let herself in, she felt a deep stillness of an empty house. Hagar wandered in, setting her purse and keys down on the dining room table. She walked down the hallway towards her mother's bedroom. The door was open; the bed was made. But no mother was there. Hagar glanced over at Bakry's room- the same. For a second Hagar wondered where they might be- then, as her heart sank, she realized it had become so commonplace she didn't even need a note from the mother to know.

`They went to the farm, without her. Again.`

The Girl
Cairo

Tension continued to build in the house between Hagar's mother and father as the mosque visits became irregular and unpredictable. Despite Hagar's father having disowned her, he still took her religious beliefs as his responsibility- except now it was a bit more sporadic than usual. He had become busy with other things, Hagar figured. Almost every Thursday night involved a fight, each evening ending in exhaustion and devastation- whether it was her father showing up out of blue and Hagar being gone somewhere to study, or whether he showed up extremely late and the family was already asleep, not at all prepared to put clothes on and go to the mosque for a late night. Part of her hated it when her parents fought- her father would yell loudly, the anger building so quickly, so strongly in his body she thought he would have a heart attack on the spot. But part of her relished the fights, hoping that eventually the mother or father would throw their hands up and declare the marriage defunct. Part of me loved the fights, because more than anything, I wanted mother to leave him. She always came back despite the frustration and tears. I never understood why. To me, it would have been a relief to leave the dysfunctional family we had become. My father had no desire to understand my mother- no desire to respect anything that differed from his idea of right. To me, he loved his religion, his God, and his afterlife more than he would ever love us.

In Middle School Hagar would cower in her room during these fights, seeking the dark warmth of her closet when the fights got bad. In high school things changed. She had no outlet for the anger building up in the house. Now during fights Hagar almost always stepped in, yelling as loudly as her father, matching his anger. Their equally violent tempers produced strained necks, protruding veins, and sweaty foreheads- ending, hours later, with migraines that would not go away. The mother would sit in silence, folding her arms tightly to her chest, her thin lips pressed together. Bakry was a faint shadow during the fights, but he always seemed to physically be present on the fringes of the conflict, as if ready to interfere at any moment. Hagar would know his physical presence- was that him sitting at the far end of the dinner table? She doesn't recall him ever saying anything during the fights, but she noticed where he placed himself. He was always by his father.

One Thursday evening, the father came home, his face beaming. One woman at the mosque had bought the perfect mosque outfit for Hagar: a *galabeyya* and *hijab*, all the way from Saudi Arabia. The colors were a deep purple, so dark it was almost black. All were seated at the dinner table when the father came home, and the mother watched with horror (and Bakry with pride) as Hagar hesitantly opened the plastic wrapping. For a moment, she admired the beauty of the cloth. Then she quickly realized what it meant, and she stopped to look up at her mother, whose eyes were icy. Hagar slowly pulled out the *galabiyya*- then, as she had feared, an eloquent headscarf for her hair. And it wasn't just any old hijab- it included a cover for the nose and mouth which would leave only Hagar's steely blue eyes showing.

"Now that she has proper clothing for the mosque, she must go twice a week, like Bakry does. She was an embarrassment to the family showing up at the mosque wearing men's western clothes. Now- she will look proper!"

Hagar never knew what made her mother snap- if it was the sight of the fabric, or her father's victorious grin. Maybe it was the niqab, and the thought of every aspect of her daughter's being hidden behind it. Right as Hagar was blooming into a woman- she was being put under wraps.

"Enough," the mother's voice was shaky with anger. "Enough of this. We are not doing this anymore."

"She MUST go to the mosque! It is her duty!"

"Like hell it is. Every time you come home, it is a fight- that drains all of us! Haven't you had enough? I said okay to one, then two lessons a week from the Sheikh. Then I said yes to one visit to the mosque a week. Now this? When will she have time to sleep?! Haven't you given up on her already! Just leave her be, take Bakry with you."

"Yeah, he would probably love to wear my niqab," Hagar smirked from the corner of the dinner table, the deep purple fabric glistening in the light.

"HAGAR! How can you listen to your mother? This is haram! You MUST go to the mosque- this is the inheritance, your legacy from your grandfather. How could you reject your family's heritage?"

"Because I am no longer part of this family- *your* family!" I yelled.

Mother and I had moved across the room, her arm over my chest as I stood in front of her. Father's eyes opened wide at my retort.

"This is MY decision to make! I am still the father here, I still provide for this family, and while you are under my roof you will do what I tell you to do!" the father spat, throwing the *galabiyya* fabric towards the pair.

"I think you gave up that right to me when you disowned me. Leave me alone. Take Bakry. I am done here."

Hagar rose to get up from the table, walking towards the father, who was standing at the end of the dinner table closest to the hallway that led to the bedrooms. The mother shook her head and put her head in her hands, bracing herself for yet another long night of arguing.

Out of nowhere, the father reached out and grabbed Hagar's hair. The grip was strong- stronger than Hagar had ever felt it before. It was the same grip the father had used many times on her upper arm and elbow when she misbehaved. He flung the other hand so high she didn't see it initially, bringing it down with brute force on her left cheek.

Hagar yelped with surprise, shying away from her father, attempting to evade both his grip and his hand. The mother stood up, and was yelling something incoherent. Bakry was standing too- but what he was planning on doing was unknown. His crippled arm lay to his side- completely useless in most situations, but especially useless now.

"Fine Hagar. FINE. You want to be rid of me, of this family? Here!" the father boomed. At this point Hagar had snaked away from his grip, and was standing by the front door, terrified. She cringed and braced herself as she prepared for the father to lunge at her- instead, he flung a piece of paper, across the dinner table.

"What are you doing? Come get it!" he yelled, angrily motioning for her to reach for it. Hagar didn't move.

Instead, the mother reached for the piece of paper, opening it up. Her expression was one of confusion- she looked up at Hagar and shoved the paper in her direction.

"It is in Arabic, I can't read it," the mother explained. Hagar reached for the paper standing on her tiptoes, still trying to keep a maximum distance between her and her father.

"It- it's a release. Allowing me to leave the country," Hagar said, her voice filled with astonishment. "This means- this means I can go to America for college?" Hagar looked up at her father. Her voice had betrayed too much happiness and relief as opposed to what Hagar supposed the desired effect was- for her to be disappointed, to cry and weep and beg and plead for her father to take her back.

Yeah. Right.

"I am finished with you," the father said.

There was an awkward silence, waiting for someone to pipe up that this was not the first time the father had decided he was rid of the daughter.

The father looked at Bakry, motioning to the bedroom. "Get ready, it's time to go to the mosque, son." Bakry bounced to his bedroom, eager to leave the tension of the situation.

Hagar folded the paper back into fours and was about to put it in her pocket when the mother reached out and snatched it from her. Without a word, the mother looked at the father, a look full of hate, and spat:

"The girl is not keeping the release. I am. If you want it back, get past me first."

Hagar almost let a wide smile take over her face. It was the first time the mother had stood up for her in a long time- probably since the incident. While Hagar had wanted to keep the release note, she immediately figured it would be more secure with the mother.

"*The girl* is not my problem. I wash my hands of her," the father said, and headed for the front door.

College Season
Cairo

"Fuck."

"What?! That was a valid play!"

Hakim was incredulously taking a sip of his coke.

"See?"

He began counting the backgammon moves on the board, retracing his steps to show Hagar how he played his roll.

Hakim was incredulously taking a sip of his coke. "See?" He began counting the backgammon moves on the board, retracing his steps to show Hagar how he played his roll.

"No, no I believe you," Hagar said.

She was staring at her laptop screen, which was tilted to one side on her lap as she balanced it with one hand while playing backgammon on the cafe table.

"It's Birmingham's tuition."

She was staring at her laptop screen, which was tilted to one side on her lap as she balanced it with one hand while playing backgammon on the cafe table. "It's Birmingham's tuition."

"Oh?" Hakim asked. "What is it? Expensive?"

"Yeah," Hagar said, her head in her hands. "Way too expensive for someone without EU citizenship."

She lifted her gaze to the backgammon board, and picked up the dice to roll her turn.

"What about London School of Design?" Hakim asked,

looking at Hagar. "Your photography show was amazing. You should seriously consider it."

"Hakim, I am not that good. It's just a pass time hobby and a way to have an arts class on my transcript. Besides, LSD is probably going to be even more expensive. How will I make a living as a photographer, anyway?" Hagar paused, thinking. " I also really want to study linguistics.It's the closest I can get to studying classic literature while also actually getting a job after I graduate."

She usually loved these late afternoons with Hakim at their favorite cafe. It had no name or signage, but built in the rounded clay style mimicking bedouin homes in the Western Desert, smooth and yellow. Hagar admired the cafe for its design- instead of trying to be western like other cafes in her neighborhood, the small nook rebelled by embracing its surroundings.

"I wish I could give you my EU status," Hakim said with a crooked smile, looking up at Hagar, contemplating his next move on the board. Hagar noticed he had rolled doubles. He would get to play twice this turn. Shit, she should as she examined her disposition on the board. Not looking good.

"You're so lucky that your mom is Greek," Hagar said.

"I mean, your mom is American," Hakim said. "America is where everyone is going for school. And you're more likely to get a scholarship there"

"Yeah..." Hagar responded, her voice trailing.

"What? You don't sound convinced" Hakim said, studying Hagar's face as she studied the backgammon board. "Your dad wrote a letter of release, right? That means you can leave the country? So you're free to go... anywhere, really."

"Yeah, he did." Hagar said. "I don't know why I am just not excited at the prospect..."

"It's just temporary," Hakim encouraged her watching her roll the dice. "Once you find something you're excited about, it will all come together."

Hagar sighed and looked out of the window, momentarily admiring the late afternoon sun setting over the pockmarked desert in front of them.

Still balancing her laptop on her lap after playing out her turn, Hagar opened a new tab, navigating to Google. What *about* American universities? She had only really considered European universities so far. Maybe they would be cheaper. Maybe easier to get into. She just wanted to make sure she could leave everything in Egypt behind.

She searched for the top ten universities in the U.S. She figured that would be a good place to start. She raised her eyebrows at the university rankings. The top ranked university was the military academy, West Point. Unusual, she thought. Before she knew it, she was clicking on the link to their home page.

Red, white and blue and images of white-gloved cadets in grey uniforms greeted her. *Defend the nation's freedom*, it said. She scrolled down to the tuition and admissions link and clicked on it. For a second, she could not believe what she read.

"It's FREE!"

Hakim looked up from the backgammon board, playing out his second move after having rolled doubles. "Free *university*?" He asked.

"Hakim, the number one university in the US is free," Hagar said slowly, continuing to scroll down the page.

"What's the catch? There has to be one," Hakim said, the tone of his voice rising in skepticism. "Wait… which university is number one? Harvard or Yale or Stanford are not free…"

"It's the military academy," she said bluntly. She looked at Hakim's expression, filled with surprise. She knew what his reaction would be…

"Which is… obviously it's not an option. What about the next one? " Hakim exclaimed as he bumped yet another one of

Hagar's pieces off of the backgammon board. When she didn't pick up the dice immediately after like she usually did, he looked up with questioningly.

"You aren't considering it, are you?" he asked, with urgency in his voice.

"I mean… why not?" Hagar asked weakly, looking up to him. "Look- here it says they need people who speak Arabic. And I would become an officer, not enlisted, so I guess I would be important- in a leadership position, I mean. And…" Hagar continued, "It would be free. I wouldn't need anyone's help financially. All I need to do is get into this school. I don't need to apply to ten different places for scholarships and all. And…" Hagar paused before continuing. "Imagine what my father's reaction would be? He would be SO mad," Hagar grinned at the thought.

Hakim raised his eyebrows, his deep coffee cream skin wrinkling with disapproval. "Hagar, how the hell would you join the U.S. Army? What would you have to do? Go to war? Go to Iraq? Come here and fight your own people?" He asked. "I know you hate it here, but you can't hate it *that* much. And joining just because it would piss off your dad is… a horrible way to treat your future," Hakim wrinkled his nose at the thought.

"I hate him that much," Hagar said bluntly, finally picking up the dice to start her turn.

"He is *not* worth throwing your life away to join the military-*any* military!" Hakim said, watching her play her turn. She brought her knocked off piece back on the board simultaneously cornering one of his pieces.

"Hakim, it's worth a try," Hagar said, shifting her laptop from her lap to the edge of the cafe table with the lid still open to the West Point admissions page. "Think of it as backup. I promise I'll apply to other schools too, okay? Ones in London too, so we can be close."

Hakim shook his head while rolling the dice, playing out his next turn. Unremarkable. He had to leave his piece open to Hagar's next turn.

```
All I could think about was how angry father
would be if I joined the United States military.
There had to be a place better than here. And I
knew what the United States stood for- all I had
to do was look at all the kids who attended youth
group. They had a choice to live the life they
were living. They could choose who they wanted
to be, what they believed in, what they wanted
to wear, who they dated… they didn't have any of
those things dictated to them. Why wouldn't I
want that? And why wouldn't I want to defend
that, even at the expense of others' lives? How
many other fathers like mine could I eliminate
from little girls' lives who were all trying to
find their way, live their lives just like I
was? It was a perfect plan, really...
```

Hagar picked up the dice after he completed his turn, blowing on her clenched fists as she shook them in her hands. If she could roll doubles, it would be…

"Match!" Hagar said triumphantly, knocking his last piece off of the board with a triumphant double roll. She gestured for another round of coals, puffing her pipe victoriously. Her sudden high spirits did not bode well, Hakim thought as they scrapped the board, preparing for another game. He knew her. Once she got an idea in her head, it was very hard for her to let it go.

Resolution

Cairo

Hagar stared at the text. She read it again, letting the words sink in before she responded. IF she responded, of course…

Grace wants to meet?

Of course you'll meet with her.

Hagar stared at the text again. Grace wanted to meet up at a shisha cafe -a brand new one that had just opened. Hagar had mentally added it to the list of cafes that her and Hakim would go to at some point… but this presented a new opportunity to go.

She clicked her phone screen off, looking away. Why did Grace want to meet now? Hagar was not in the mood to fight. She had also received the text earlier in the day and still had not responded. At some point… she would have to do something.

She finally clicked the phone screen back on, swiping to unlock it. She looked up, deep in thought. How to sound not too eager…?

She finally typed: "Sounds good. I'll head over there in about an hour." She hit send. She quickly clicked the screen off and leaned back in her chair.. Hagar jumped up from her desk eagerly and looked at her closet. She needed to change out of her sweaty school clothes.

Minutes later, Hagar was walking to the cafe. It was later in the day, her favorite part of the evening. It was that time when everything appeared to be basked in golden light, slanted, coming in from the west. All the trees appeared to be resting in relief after a hot day, with the deep darker shadows between the branches pressing into rest while the few leaves on the surface seemed to wave the sun away. The flatness of the hot midday sun suddenly waning, other parts of the city seemed to come alive- stray dogs and cats basked on the sidewalks after hiding in the shade all day. Butterflies floated about blooming bushes. Everyone who was walking home from work had a brisker, livelier step than the lunch crowd, cooled by the slight breeze that blew down the streets that acted like narrow, concrete corridors.

Hagar arrived at the cafe, almost missing its green arch amongst all the trees. She opened the gate and stood breathless, taking in the setup. Elevated verandahs stood on her left and right, forming small circular seating areas in a popular bedouin style. Each seating area was private, made of what looked like sand-colored clay. Each seating had a low table that emerged from the smooth clay at the center. The top pointed like a teepee, with dried reeds woven together. They strung each seating area with Christmas lights and Ramadan lanterns, each panel of the lantern a stained glass piece of different colors. The ambiance was calm, the only lighting that appeared protruded from the Ramadan lamps; a warm yellow light tinted with various shades of reds, blues and greens. Geometric shapes formed the sides of the lanterns, and their designs projected outwards on the walls, creating small shapes for the flies to lazily dance from one to the other. Arabic style coffee shop music cooed from the speakers. Hagar inspected each seating area, looking for Grace.

"Hagar!"

Hagar looked up and saw Grace seated at one of the verandahs. As Hagar approached, she noticed the benches were lined with colorful, soft hand made rag rugs. Under the rugs were seat cushions, softening the cold feel of the clay beneath them. Hagar stepped into the verandah and took a seat in the shallow bench across from Grace, folding her feet to sit cross-legged.

"Hey, Grace," Hagar said, sinking into the cushions. A waiter approached, placing a menu in front of her.

"Shisha, madame?" he inquired.

Hagar nodded. "Let's try watermelon." She looked inquisitively at Grace. She knew Grace didn't smoke, but wasn't sure if she would order something considering she had picked the place being a shisha cafe.

Grace waved away the offer. "I'll wait to order food, thank you. Just lemonade with mint for me, please." The waiter nodded and stepped down from the verandah.

Hagar pulled her backpack around next to her. It had zipped open slightly, revealing her biology textbook. Grace grimaced.

"How is biology going for you? It's kicking my ass. I really could use a study buddy you know," she said, gesturing at the textbook.

Hagar raised an eyebrow. "I am sure there are plenty of people who would be happy to study with you... Shams included," Hagar responded pointedly.

One big happy family reunion..

Grace shook her head. "He is too smart. He doesn't study with anybody. He just... knows this shit. Without even trying. Totally not my pace," Grace said, smiling at the thought of Shams. Hagar winced. The conversation had started off uncomfortably. As her shisha arrived, the waiter placed it on the table in front of Hagar. She admired the unique presentation- the pipe was stuck into an actual watermelon, where the water was stored. The waiter had placed a leather corded placemat to hold the watermelon in place. After testing the coals, Hagar ordered a cold mint juice. The waiter nodded and was off.

Hagar inhaled the sweet smoke, molasses and watermelon filling her lungs. The smoke tasted sweeter and more concentrated- Hagar smiled in appreciation at the watermelon, patting it with satisfaction.

"You know all I needed was an apology," Grace snapped.

Hagar looked away from her shisha, giving Grace an incredulous, blank stare. What?

"All you needed was… an apology?" Hagar asked. "Grace, I apologized to you. For multiple things that happened. That changed nothing." Deep inhale.

"I mean- I needed a sincere apology. That one felt like you were blaming me for stuff. Honestly, that is all I would need and we would have been good months ago."

"Oh, that and Shams back," Hagar spat.

Grace blushed. "We were just on a break, you know," she stammered. "When things happened between you guys. But anyway… we aren't together anymore. We tried. It just didn't work."

"Why? Maybe because he went for your best friend the moment you left?"

"And my best friend fell for my ex-boyfriend! It goes both ways!"

Hagar shook her head. She turned her attention to the waiter, who had made his looming presence known. "Food, madames?" he asked. Hagar and Grace nodded. It appeared the cafe specialized in wood-fired pizza. Hagar and Grace split a large fig and gorgonzola pizza with hot honey. Hagar finally looked up from the menu and took another inhale of her shisha. "Look, Grace, what do you want? This all happened a while ago. Why talk now? Why rehash all of this now? We are all going to graduate soon and go our separate ways, then we can forget this entire experience ever happened to us."

"Because it matters to me," Grace said. "Your friendship. I never wanted to lose you."

Hagar raised her eyebrows. So many things she wanted to blame Grace for. Of not being there. Of ignoring Hagar's puppy-dog-like presence while Grace dated Shams. How she never reached out when Hagar went radio silent at the start of her and Shams' relationship. Of the accusations Grace flung her way when Grace found out about her father's second wife… the list went on. Hagar pushed these feelings back with a deep gulp.

She wants to be friends again. Get over yourself.

Yeah but at what expense? It's not like she was a great friend to begin with… all the things…

But think of all the things she DID support you through… the countless fights at home, the many sleepovers to escape from them.

She probably just wants to be friends again because she and Shams didn't work out…

Well. Beggars can't be choosers.

Hagar looked up from fiddling with her fingers to meet Grace's gaze.

"Okay, Grace. Fine. Here is your apology- I apologize for everything."

There was a hesitant silence that hung between them. What more does she want?

Grace paused for a moment, then a big smile crept across her face. She nodded in satisfaction and took a sip of her cold lemonade. And just like that, the two slipped into casual conversation until their pizza arrived.

See- now at least you have SOMEONE on your side.

Hagar smiled widely as they ate. She chewed on the melted cheesy bread with satisfaction, looking up at the geometric shapes from the lanterns that had grown deeper and longer as evening shadows crept in to take over the faint sun's rays. She savored the taste of warm fig and cheese as she watched fruit flies lazily buzz around the lanterns, counting the small triangles on the wall.

No.
Cairo

Hagar stared at the piece of paper.

Hagar Khalifa. Your name is clearly different. What will you do if you're treated differently because of it?

"Well, hon, what does it say?" her mother asked. Judging by Hagar's eyes changing to a deeper shade of gray, she concluded she might already know the answer.

"Yeah, Hagar. Is the US Army going to admit a brown girl like you?" Bakry jeered from the corner of the red and white checkered restaurant table. The mother knocked the top of his arm with her fist.

Hagar put the paper face down and reached for another piece of pizza. She was quiet.

The mother sighed and looked at her daughter. She knew the news of whether West Point had admitted her would arrive any day- once the mother picked up the envelope, she had booked dinner reservations their favorite Italian restaurant around the corner from the house. Pizza was always a sure way to cheer the girl up if the news was bad, or celebrate if the news was good.

The mother had mixed feelings about Hagar applying to West Point. Not only was she worried about how many lies she would have to spin to keep Hagar's father clueless - she felt the move to a military academy was incompatible with Hagar's desire for independence. With who Hagar was.

She would just be moving from one dictatorship to another.

"Hagar, say something!" Bakry said. Hagar looked at his twinkling brown eyes.

"They wouldn't take a brown Egyptian chick, you're right, you idiot," Hagar spat.

The mother reached to place her hand on Hagar's gently. "Honey, it's okay. You have so many other options! Maybe now we can try to figure out a way to get you to the University of Birmingham? It's so much closer to us. We will figure out the cost, don't worry," the mother said, patting Hagar's hand. "They seem to have a great linguistics program."

"Or, Hagar could just stay in Egypt with her family and go to Cairo University," Bakry said. "Baba gets free tuition because he lectures there. They also have a great linguistics department there".

"Bakry, *please...*" the mother sighed heavily.

"I would never stay here to study." Hagar said pointedly, directing her retort at Bakry.

"Pizza! Eat pizza! Enough," the mother said. Hagar played with frozen droplets of wax on the gob of candles sitting at the table, one melted atop of the other. The wax embraced an empty broken red wine bottle-that danced with echoes of the red, velvety liquid that once occupied it every time the candle's light hit it from above.

"They offered me a scholarship instead," Hagar said at last, breaking the silence. "Something called a Reserve Officer Training Corps active duty scholarship."

The mother's eyes lit up, and she squeezed Hagar's hand. "What does this mean?"

"It means that I wasn't good enough for the academy, but the Army will still pay for me to go to school anywhere else in America provided I enroll in this program."

The mother smiled widely. "So, a normal university? With all expenses paid?"

"Yes, ma."

"Honey, that's great!" the mother said. "That's a full ride scholarship!" She elbowed Bakry in the ribs as he took a bite of pizza.

He coughed, swallowing the rest of his bite, and growled at the mother sideways. "Great, so she wasn't good enough, but the Army is desperate for Arabic speakers and will let her in anyway."

"There is no winning with you, Bakry." The mother sighed, exasperated.

Hagar shook her head. "He's right. I'm second-rate. Just barely good enough. But at least I can go to college," she huffed.

"I don't understand why you hate Egypt so much. You have your family here. You have the farm. Your roots and culture. Why would you want to leave?" Bakry said.

"Because I hate it here. I hate everything about here," Hagar said.

"Someday, Hagar, you'll end up right back here, right back where you started. And then I will get to say I told you so," Bakry said, stuffing a bite of pizza in his mouth.

Hagar looked Bakry in the eye, reaching for a piece of pizza, and said:

"Never."

The Life She Could Have Had
Cairo

Hagar pushed the apartment door open, finding it unlocked. Unusual, since her mother was at work and Bakry was likely at after school Quran lessons at the mosque. As she entered, her father greeted her sitting at the dining room table with a man she had never seen before.

"Hagar, finally you have come home!" the father said. He was unusually cheerful this afternoon. Hagar looked at the guest, slightly aghast. Did mom know he was here? Since when did she allow guests in the house?

"Yes, dad... I always come home," Hagar responded, annoyed at his cheerful facade.

It looked like her dad was tutoring the strange man- books were on the table and Hagar could see anatomy charts unfolded in front of them. Hagar recalled him bringing students home all the time when she was very young. The mother would always make them tea and welcome them. She told Hagar lessons were to earn extra money to help buy the farm. As the kids grew older, tutoring lessons at home stopped altogether.

It was also unusual for her father to be home at all. He had only intermittently appeared to pick up Bakry to go to the mosque. The occasional fight. But not tutoring at the dinner table. This was the most comfortable Hagar had ever seen the father in their home.

Her father motioned her to come to the table and greet their guest. Hagar shook her head, rolled her eyes, and instead turned to head down the hallway, her backpack still slung on her shoulder.

"Baba, I have a lot of homework to do tonight. Sorry I can't say hi."

"Nonsense Hagar, you can spare a few minutes to say hello to Karim. He is one of my students from the university."

Hagar did not move from where she had stopped in front of the kitchen. She gave a nod at Karim.

"See my daughter, how beautiful she is?" the father crooned, gesturing at Hagar. "You wouldn't even know she is my daughter! Everyone says she looks like a khawaga, but she speaks and reads and writes Arabic very well!"

Hagar rolled her eyes. This routine was familiar- the father did it at the mosque, all the men drooling over Hagar's foreign appearance. Boasting about how light her skin was, how blue Hagar's eyes were and how her curls were like honey being poured out of a jar. People never thought she was his daughter because of her light her features. Bakry rarely received this kind of attention. Hagar looked around.

"Where *is* Bakry?" she asked out loud.

"He is in his room, studying," the father said. "Hagar, join us at the table now." Hagar slowly walked to the table and sat down. Maybe if I sit down and talk a bit, this will pass and I can go to my room.

"Karim here is a first-year student," her father said, gesturing towards Karim. "His parents are university benefactors, and have been very generous towards my department. Karim is your age, you know."

Hagar looked at Karim closely. There was nothing special about his appearance. He had a narrow, hawkish face and a pointed nose. He was extremely skinny. His skin was lighter than even hers. A light splash of freckles across his face. His hair stood straight up in a curly flat top. He clearly groomed every morning based on the generous amounts of product in his dark curls.

"Hi Karim," Hagar said flatly in the boy's direction.

"You know, Hagar, maybe you and Karim can go to dinner sometime?" the father suggested.

Hagar looked at him wide-eyed. Dad wants me to go to dinner with… a boy? "Dad, I am going to America for college. That would be silly," Hagar said.

Hagar's father smiled uneasily. "We haven't decided on America, Hagar. Besides, dinner wouldn't hurt?"

Hagar looked at Karim again. His polite smile frozen in place, his eyes showing no particular embarrassment or excitement. Hagar shook her head.

He wants you to go on a date…

Probably has more than that in mind.

Already in medical school. He is already all set. If this isn't an arranged marriage setup, I don't know what it is.

And is that so bad?

Are you kidding? I have to get out of here. Even if that means the plan changes a bit. If I go on a date, it's all over, I'll be under my father's thumb for the rest of my life…

You have been resisting that… but how do you know it will be better over there?

"Hagar Khalifa. Your name is clearly from somewhere else. What will you do if you're treated differently because of it?"

I don't, okay. But anything is better than here… anything.

"Are we done here?" Hagar asked the father abruptly with the thought of the failed West Point interview. She stood up and grabbed her school bag. "I have homework to do."

Her father shook his head and stood. "Fine, Hagar, go to your room," he said sternly, following her into the hallway.

"Excellent," Hagar retorted under her breath as she picked up her backpack and headed down the hallway.

The hair stood up on her neck slowly as she walked to her room. She could feel her father following her.

"Hagar, you are very rude in front of visitors. That is no way for my daughter to act," he hissed. "Someday, you will marry a good Muslim man. And you will live here, in Egypt, with your family. Even if you and your mother send you to college- I don't care, you *will* come back home."

Hagar scowled. "What happened to disowning me? To not caring?" she retorted.

"Go to college, Hagar." Her body reverberated as he jerked her arm with his tight grip. "But you will be back."

The father turned to leave Hagar's room and slammed the door behind him. Hagar slumped to a seat on the edge of her bed.

If I might say…

Shut up.

For a moment, Hagar felt a deep wave of loneliness wash over her chest and heart.

My father gave up on me.

But if you went to dinner with Karim…

That life is not meant for me.

But the Army is? Hagar, are you certain where you're going is better than where you came from?

Hagar paused.

It has to be.

The Virginian
Mokattam Heights

Perched on the edge of the Mokattam cliffs, the Virginian had a perfect view of the city's skyline. The restaurant and bar was an old relic with hints of the British empire's hold on the country during the 1940s. It was one of the few restaurants in the area that served alcohol, water pipes, and food all in one location. Hagar always imagined it as an old bar or saloon for British soldiers and diplomats. Chipped, dirty statues of horses on pillars lined the outdoor seating area, with a stage placed in the back for weddings and ceremonies. She and Hakim were usually one of a handful of customers there. It would be so quiet, they could hear the roar of traffic below them in the busy city.

Hagar and Hakim had agreed it was high time to pay a visit to the Virginian. Both were leaving for college that summer; a final romp around town was in order. A feeling of nostalgia cloaked the night rumbling up the cliff on ill-paved roads.

Their waiter appeared at the end of the table shortly after they sat down.

"*Mas'aa el kheir*, mister and madame, what would you like to drink today?" the waiter asked with one arm behind him. His crisp white collared shirt and blue and white striped apron seemed overdone in the restaurant's shabbiness that only echoed of luxury past. Hakim ordered a Sakarra beer, and so did Hagar. They also ordered shisha.

"So… it's decided? Colorado?" Hakim asked, eager to hear about Hagar's recent biggest decision.

"Yes," she exhaled softly, looking over her shoulder at the view below. "It seemed the best of the choices I had left. I didn't apply to many colleges outside of West Point as you know…"

Hakim nodded. "It seems like a good choice. Colorado is beautiful, Hagar- you will love it there. Minus the Army program of course!" Hakim stuck out his tongue in jest. Hagar made a face at him. She knew he still had reservations about the Army program- secretly, so did she- but she was going to prove him wrong.

`I will prove them all wrong.`

The waiter brought their water pipes. Hakim tried his immediately, inhaling deeply, letting out a smooth, white cloud of smoke. Smoke swirled from his nose and his mouth, creating a relaxing cloud of mist around his head.

Hagar inhaled, drawing in the sticky mustiness. She looked out over the small ledge down at the city. To the right, she could see the bright white and green lights of the Salah Al Din mosque. Next to the mosque was a pool of lights, likely coming from the crowded Khan El Khalili market. To the left was complete darkness.

"It's crazy how there are no lights in the City of the Dead," Hagar mused aloud.

Hakim looked out, his dark brown eyes reflecting the lights of the city below him. "It really looks dead- like nothing lives there."

They both knew better. The City of the Dead. They had been through the winding pathways multiple times. A community had formed in the vast Islamic Cairo cemetery, housing one of the largest slums in the world. Inside every family plot that had a wall, or a structure built, a family crouched under makeshift lean-to's that housed upwards of ten. Children would play hide and seek amongst the headstones, running over the bodies above and below. Small stands selling water and sodas were erected haphazardly through the narrow, winding walkways in between plots.

"I still don't understand the Army thing," Hakim finally said. "But hopefully you find it to be what you are hoping for."

"I hope so too," she said, looking at Hakim with uncertainty

Hagar Khalifa. Your name is clearly different. What will you do if you're treated differently because of it?

"We're going to miss this," said Hakim, looking at Hagar.

"I know. It has been hard, but I know I will miss it," she said, looking down at her beer.

"You don't really think that," Hakim said knowingly. "But you will miss your family. Even your dad."

Hagar rolled her eyes. "I doubt that- he is the reason I am leaving!" She tossed her curls to the side dismissively.

"We'll see… you know Egypt has a way of calling people back home" he said with a twinkle in his eye.

Escape
Cairo Airport

Hagar looked out the white Jeep passenger window as they bumped down the highway. The morning light was creeping over the desert, an angry orange peering through the half-open eyelids of the early dawn sky. Hagar breathed in deeply. There was a smell to the air of Cairo this far out into the desert when there was no traffic. It smelled like morning dew droplets with particles of sand mixing. Not quite like fresh soil, but something close to it.

She watched as the windows on tall apartment buildings glinted in the indirect sunlight. Her father had once explained to her how apartment values priced based on which cardinal direction they faced. *Bahary*, or a view with windows facing north, was the desired direction. *Bahr* is the Arabic word for sea, the expression referring to the cool breezes believed to reach Cairo from the Mediterranean in the North.

"Hagar, what are you thinking about?" her mother asked from the driver's seat.

Hagar faced her mother. The mother's dirty blonde wavy hair was especially active this morning, flowing with the breeze that came through the driver's window that was slightly cracked open. Her eyes were light, the sunlight tickling the deep blue pockets that striped her iris. But deep lines of worry were pressed around her eyes and lips.

"Nothing, ma," Hagar said, pressing her mother's hand on the Jeep's gear shift.

Hagar felt a pang deep in her chest. It was new, this pain. She had never stopped to notice it before. Or maybe she had never slowed down enough to know it would come. The pang she felt was a mixture of the fear she had felt for months. Excitement and anticipation. Eagerness to leave Egypt behind her.

But this pang was different. She was missing her mother already. Then- she realized- she was missing more than that.

She missed her mother's face as her hair blew across it in the wind.

She missed the wind tickling her own face as they rode on the backs of horses.

She missed the firm grip of her mother's hand on her own whenever times got tough.

She missed the sunrise- how especially colorful they always were in Egypt.

She missed the desert. The sand was always quiet, yet its waves told soft stories. The flat horizon made Hagar feel she could see the entire world.

She would miss the starry farm sky, the milky way clear as day.

She even found herself missing her father... for a moment, fleeting.

Hagar reached up to open the Jeep door as they pulled into their favorite breakfast place near the pyramids. They decided it was the perfect place to go before she left.

"The usual?" Hagar asked, looking at her mother.

"The usual," the mother smiled and nodded. Instead of reaching into her pocket to give Hagar money, Hagar slipped out of the car and grabbed her wallet. She had saved $500 for the trip, and planned on spending the last bit of Egyptian money on this breakfast.

Hagar looked around as she waited in the familiar line. The

early morning bustle was the same- the young boys chopping vegetables, yelling, stable hands jostling against her yelling their orders in. A sweet smell of fava beans being mashed and fried with onions, garlic, and peppers. The *taa'miya* patties making snapping and bubbling sounds in the deep fryer. Nothing had changed. Hagar waited patiently, thinking of nothing and busying her mind with watching those around her going about their usual morning. Everything seemed so normal for them- and so abnormal for her.

She paid for the sandwiches and returned to the Jeep, slumping in the front seat. She handed her mother a mushy sandwich and set the other on the dash. Hagar stared at the storefront quietly, still taking in all the activity around it. As if it would be the last time.

"Hagar, it is going to be okay," the mother said, squeezing Hagar's hand. "I'm sorry we had to do it this way. But it's better. Less complicated."

Hagar looked down in sadness. For the first time her heart filled with doubt.

"What if this is the wrong thing?" Hagar asked. "What if everything I've chosen for myself is wrong? What if I'm meant to stay?"

Her mother shook her head. "Hagar, you were never meant to stay."

"But ma, I want to be with you. And dad…"

"Don't worry about dad.. I can handle him."

"I know, but I still feel like I'm abandoning you."

"Hagar, you are starting your *life*. The life you chose for *you*. You are not abandoning us- you are doing what you are supposed to do! Living!"

Hagar looked back at the sunrise. It was growing brighter and brighter as they drove along the highway, away from the pyramids towards the airport.

"But what if I was wrong?" Hagar repeated the question.

"What if this future I have chosen for myself is wrong?"

"Honey, you won't know until you get there," her mother said. "There will be good times and bad. You will make choices you wish you hadn't made. You will make mistakes. But don't worry- I am here."

Hagar imagined her mother at the farm. She was stroking the area around the eyes of a roan mare speckled with pinkish flecks, softly cupping her hands around their large dark almond shapes. The sunlight was soft on the mother and mare's faces, bent towards one another. The mare was calm, pushing ever so lightly into the mother's palm as it ran over her eye, again and again. The mare's forelock was blowing in the wind. Mother's eyes were quiet, her lips lingering. Hagar couldn't quite hear what the mother was saying- the wind was too loud. She heard soft murmurs in the singsong voice the mother would use talking to calm down the horses.

Hagar looked at her mother's face. The two had decided, weeks prior, that they would book Hagar's tickets for America without telling her father or Bakry. The mother didn't want to risk of the father changing his mind at the last minute.

Hagar then realized the pang in her chest was not just missing her mother- it was also fear. What if father got angry when he found out? What would happen? And where in the hell was she going?

"Hagar, I can handle him," the mother insisted, as if reading her thoughts. "Everything will be fine."

They were pulling up to the airport terminal. Hagar glanced at the backseat, checking on her bags, making sure they were still there. Instead, her vision was of her and Bakry, much younger, much smaller, sitting on the benches giggling at one another. She shook her head as if to rid her mind of the image.

"Hagar, I have something to give you. Or give back to you, rather," the mother said, pulling Hagar's attention back. Hagar looked at her mother's face, then down at her hands. A small velvety jewelry box was in her palm. Hagar reached for it and opened it gingerly. Her eyes lit up initially, then darkened again. She stared at the contents of the box a moment, then looked at her mother, snapping it shut.

"Thank you, ma. You did what you promised," Hagar smiled weakly.

"I know faith has stung you," the mother said, placing a hand over the jewelry box in the palm of Hagar's hand. "But I promise, if you stick with your journey, someday you will find the answer."

Hagar nodded.

Part of me believed her- or wanted to, seeing that old familiar heart and cross pendant mother had gifted me so many years ago. Had she given me the necklace prior to the incident, I might have celebrated with joy. It felt like every step I took until I got on that plane was filled with dread, as if I would wake up and suddenly be back in my childhood bedroom with my father rapping his knuckles on the door telling me to get ready to go to the mosque. The pendant didn't give me relief that morning in the Jeep- it felt like something that had failed me. A promise that went wrong. A promise unfulfilled.

Hagar placed the jewelry box in her purse, glancing down to check one more time and make sure she had her new U.S. passport and her plane ticket printed.

The mother and Hagar stepped out of the Jeep and unloaded the suitcases onto a cart.

"I can't go in with you," the mother said, her voice shaky. Hagar understood. This was goodbye, and the mother was doing everything she could to hold it together.

"Ma..." Hagar said- then she was speechless.

The mother threw her arms around her daughter, engulfing

her in blonde wavy hair. Hagar wrapped her arms around her mother's body, squeezing her as hard as she could.

Maybe I didn't want to leave.

They looked deep into each other's eyes, sets of blue and grey, glassy with the pressure of repressed tears, hoping none would spill out.

"Ma, I love you, always," Hagar whispered.

"Darling, I love you too, always," the mother said, squeezing the daughter's shoulders. "Now, go catch your flight, your life is waiting for you!" The mother grabbed Hagar's shoulders, turning her around to face the airport entrance.

Hagar began pushing the cart robotically towards the door. The military guard looked at her brand new American passport and paper ticket. Hagar held her breath as he inspected it.

"Where were you born?" the guard asked.

"Here, in Egypt," Hagar said, fidgeting with the card that held her three suitcases.

"You are less than 21 years old. Where is your father?" the guard asked, looking at Hagar's mother, who stood by the Jeep with her arms crossed.

"I have a note of release from him," Hagar offered, pulling the note out of her backpack. The guard scrutinized it.

"Where are you going?" he asked her, staring at her mere three suitcases then towards the Jeep.

"I am going to America. For college," she said.

The guard took a moment, looking at the girl, then back at her passport. He flipped the passport shut, tucked the note inside of it, and looked at the girl quizzically.

"Strange, a girl this young going to America alone," he said. "*Bon voyage*." He gestured her through the doors into the terminal.

Hagar took one more look back at her mother, and nodded. She was in. She was leaving.

The mother was far enough away that Hagar likely wouldn't

see her tears. She couldn't control them anymore anyway.

Hagar waved at her mother through the terminal window. She saw her mother hop in the Jeep, turn on the engine, and pause, her forehead falling down to the top of the steering wheel. Hagar could see her mother's back rise and fall with sobs. She spun away, her own eyes filling with tears.

Hagar took a deep breath, closing her eyes.

`Okay. Life starts now.`

And she stepped through the security gate.

About The Author

Amina Al Sherif is the author of the *Nadiri* fiction series. Originally from Cairo, Egypt, she immigrated to the United States in 2010 as a first-generation Arab and African American. Amina is a member of the LGBTQ+ community and is a US Army veteran. Amina lives in the San Antonio, Texas area with her daughter Amal and her German Shepherd, DFO. By day, Amina is a machine learning engineer at Google.

Note From Amina Al Sherif

Word-of-mouth is crucial for any author to succeed. If you enjoyed *Nadiri*, please leave a review online — anywhere you are able. Even if it's just a sentence or two. It would make all the difference and would be very much appreciated.

Thanks!
Amina Al Sherif

We hope you enjoyed reading this title from:

www.blackrosewriting.com

Subscribe to our mailing list – *The Rosevine* – and receive **FREE** books, daily deals, and stay current with news about upcoming releases and our hottest authors. Scan the QR code below to sign up.

Already a subscriber? Please accept a sincere thank you for being a fan of Black Rose Writing authors.

View other Black Rose Writing titles at www.blackrosewriting.com/books and use promo code **PRINT** to receive a **20% discount** when purchasing.

www.ingramcontent.com/pod-product-compliance
Lightning Source LLC
Chambersburg PA
CBHW030855200726
48289CB00003B/757